I0535848

Medical Kit from Central State Hospital for the Insane

Photo by James Ward Kirk

Indiana Horror Review 2015

Book © 2015 James Ward Kirk Publishing

Internet: http://www.jwkfiction.com
Twitter: @jameswardkirk
Facebook: James-Ward-Kirk-Fiction

Cover art © John D. Stanton 2015
Cover Design by John D. Stanton

ISBN-13: 978-0692572528 (James Ward Kirk Publishing)

ISBN-10: 069257252X

All rights reserved. No part of this book may be reproduced in any form or by any electronic or mechanical means, including information storage and retrieval systems, without written permission from the publisher or author, except in the case of a reviewer, who may quote brief passages embodied in critical articles or in a review.

Contents

Jennifer Lemming Charmed...1

K.Z. Morano Zhang Jian and the Sandman 10

William Cook A Dream Realized.....................................24

Mike Jansen The View from Distant Aeons.....................30

Roger Cowin The Watcher in the Dark 45

A. Henry Keene Bailey...54

A. Henry Keene Little Girl Lost.......................................60

A. Henry Keene Painted Tusk of Mastodon 61

Flo Stanton A Small Talent 63

Justin Hunter Wrong Blood Type....................................70

Dona Fox Last Chance in Lafayette A Love Story............79

Maria Mitchell The Lake Michigan Triangle....................91

Sebastian Crow Loving the Dead 93

Sebastian Crow Cemetery Ghosts...................................103

Maria Mitchell White Commodore..................................105

Sebastian Crow The Watchful Dead 107

A. Henry Keene Tangled...108

Guy Burtenshaw All in the Preparation 109

Bas van deR Veer   The firefighter 118

Alec Cizak   Worms 123

Mary Patterson Thornburg   Tricker-Treat 132

John D. Stanton   Zero-point 137

Author Bios 145

Jennifer Lemming

Charmed

The bees wait for her, for their charmer, to gather their honey. Others have gathered it before her, for theirs was an old hive nestled in a tree trunk. The path to the trunk has worn down over many years, and now the girl who gathers honey takes the same path to their hive. She loves the bees and honey gathering more than any other charmer. The daughters of the Queen can sense her coming, from afar, even though she may be at the far edge of the apple orchard, and the bees buzz with happiness when she crosses the field of clover that covers the ground to their hive. With the other charmers, they sometimes sense fear, sometimes resolution. They only felt her joy and, in their happiness, they try to match their buzzing to her tone to the rhythm of her beating heart.

To the bees, even her skin seems like a fine honeycomb, over which they gladly crawl, sensing the warm red sap that flows under her skin. If they sting her, which happens only rarely, she never slaps at them. She seems to accept it as part of the process, never jerking or hissing in fear or anger. In that way, she is not like the others. When she gathers honey, she breaks off the combs with care and gently tastes the nectar. She radiates gratitude. The drones sense their Queen has much respect for the Charmer, and she allows her drones their individual love for the Charmer. The bees, in turn love their Queen even more for that privilege. So intense the time spent with their Charmer, that each time she finishes harvesting the hive and departs, they ache from her absence and buzz sorrow in the empty space she left behind.

This became the routine for the bees: the gathering nectar and enjoying the visits from the charmer, freely giving up their creation that the charmer calls honey. The nights are uneventful with creatures of the forest that roam when the warm loving orb, the sun sets. One night there was a creature roaming the forest that had no red sap. It radiated an angry thirst but the hive understood from their Queen that the creature's thirst was not a danger for them. They then buzzed about with disinterest.

There was this day when their Charmer was crossing the field of clover. She stopped before she got to the hive and looked over a low field below, at a man in a nearby apple orchard. The bees were confused because while they sensed her happiness, she didn't seem to notice them at all. Their Charmer turned her face from the hive, toward the man, and the bees sense they would have to share their Charmer's happiness with him. Though she was still her carefree self, the bees sensed she was distracted with joy. A few bees buzzed with jealousy, a new emotion for the Hive.

Several days passed this way with the Charmer looking for the man in the orchard before reaching the hive. One particular day the bees sensed that she wasn't as happy as the other days. She walked more slowly this time, and she neither stopped nor looked for the man as she had done before. She continued straight to the hive, her face tilted away from the sun. The bees around the hive buzzed with the knowledge that their Charmer was now sad, and as they buzzed around her, they felt the slower vibrations of her heart.

The Charmer continued to go to the hive in her same sad mood for several days, but always she showed her love to the bees, though now muted. The bees sensed something wrong but were unable to understand her sadness, so they buzzed more softly whenever she was near, and they felt her unhappiness soften.

Their Charmer now often lingered at the Hive, with no hurry to return to the village. Waiting until the sun hung low in the sky, the bees and their Queen simply enjoyed her presence, even muted by melancholy.

She stayed very long into the afternoon one day. Perhaps, the bees thought, she now preferred their company to her humans. She startled, though, as the crease of the day started to fold into night. The bees also sensed the presence of the creature with no red sap, as their Charmer ran toward her village in the growing darkness with worry and alarm.

A few days later, the day after the night of the New Moon, they noticed that she was not herself when she visited the hive that day. They sensed that her body was weaker, and she was less thoughtful, which confused them. When she reached the end of the orchard and work her way slowly through the clover they sensed she had less energy than before.

Her skin, which they loved to crawl over, was colder, and she didn't hum with her sunny melodies. She did not seem happy to see them, using all her energy to harvest the honey. One of the bees, the one who especially who loved to crawl on her skin, buzzed through her hair, landed on her neck, and crawled over two puncture wounds on their Bee Charmer's neck. This bee tasted the iron in the dried blood dried around the wounds. He sent the information to the other bees, including the Queen. The Queen's message was that, through these wounds, the Charmer's energy, her red sap, was stolen.

When the Bee Charmer had left them for the day, they turned to their Queen, who seemed puzzled. They sensed something from their Queen that they had never before felt from her: sadness.

The Bee Charmer's energy, more slowly with each visit, diminished. She began to wear her clothing so that it covered her paling complexion. Despite this the bees still craved to touch her and leaving a trace of their nectar on her skin and hair. She started to wear a wide brim hat, and the bees noticed her aversion to the sun, the warm orb that meant their very life. They did not understand her fear. It slowly became clear to the bees there was something new in her: darkness.

The bees buzzed around the Bee Charmer. The honey gathering had gone badly one particular day. The Bee Charmer, more heavily covered than ever before, swatted the bees away with anger. She had done something she had never done before. She left with no hint of gratefulness. The entire hive buzzed that night with confusion, hurt, and sadness.

In the days that followed, the Charmer didn't return. The bees buzzed with an ache, an ache of not knowing, of emptiness. On the third sunrise after her last visit, the male that had charmed their Charmer, full of fear and sadness, came to their hive and tacked a piece of paper to the tree above the hive. He then left quickly, the bees leaving him with a few choice stings.

The bees were abuzz with confusion. In their disarray, the Queen dispatched a few scouts to the house, where the charmer and her family lived. There they saw the Bee Charmer lying supine in a wooden box, candles lit, even though it was day. They swarmed all around her. She was lying so still. The house, effused with the pungent scent of a bulb plant the bees pollinated in the garden, the room filled with the dried bulbs of the Garlic plant hanging heavily all about, even from the necks of all the people present.

The Bee scouts murmured in confusion. Now they knew that the red sap that had been in the Bee Charmer was gone. One of the scouts landed on her; he was the bee who loved her the most. He landed on her still form and lightly crawled over her. Picking his way over her skin, weaving through her long, black raven hair, he then came to her skin, which was the palest hue the bees had ever known, with no hint of the red sap beneath her skin.

4

The entire hive droned their low hum of sadness as their Queen told them that the Charmer was gone and they realized she would visit them no more. The bee scout who had loved the charmer the most stayed behind, despite the strong pull of the hive and their Queen.

A rough hand struck out at him, knocking him to the wood floor, a booted foot ground him into the floor. The other four scouts buzzed away with fear and loneliness, returning to the safety of their hive.

The days now passed into the dull routine of searching out nectar, pollinating, and returning to the hive. No one in the Charmer's family had come to harvest the bee's honey. The bees hummed a lonely gratefulness, a time to be on their own. Some of the forest animals came to sample the honey produced, which now tasted like sweet grief.

Later, the hive scouts witnessed the procession of humans bearing the small, wood box that carried their charmer. The scouts followed the procession to where the humans put their dead, in a field of flat, upright stones, shaped by human hands. The scouts transmitted confusion when, instead of putting their Charmer in a hole in the ground near the entrance of this field for the dead, the group of humans had carried their charmer to the back of this field, to the part wild and tangled.

The humans placed her body in a stone crypt, and the scouts buzzed with agitation as the scent of human fear and repulsion and sadness increased until, with mercy, their Queen called them back to the hive. They quickly left this place of human decay.

Again, the days and nights passed, the clock of the earth moving toward the next New Moon.

The bees felt the new moon rise just over the horizon, just beyond the sunset. It was the first New Moon since the death of their Charmer. Now, for the first time since her death, they suddenly sensed her presence in the far distance to the West, in the field of upright stones.

She first appeared to them a few hours later, where the orchard met the field clover leading to the bee's hive. They sensed her standing there at the edge of the western stone fence, but she wasn't as before. The bees knew the red sap didn't flow in her.

They sensed in her longing, a desperate desire to gather the honey again. They had sensed such creatures before, but always at a far distance, for those like her were not hungry for sweetness of life from honey but from the red sap that flows in other living creatures. Her dark need for life radiated from her as they buzzed cautiously near. They could also taste her love of them, how she missed gathering their honey. Go to her, said their Queen. She doesn't want our honey anymore, but she will not hurt you. Therefore, the hive swarmed their Bee Charmer.

This happened night after night. The first few nights the Charmer met the hive at the edge of the western fence, arising from her stone home in the field of carved stones. The hive would swarm her, crawling all over her very cold, different skin. Where here skin had reminded them before of their warm combs, it was now colder and more tightly knit, but even frozen the bees could still sense the pattern that was only their charmer.

Together, using the hive as a living, buzzing shroud the Charmer traveled with the bees deep through the woods, and away from the village. Sensing the painful hunger that radiated from her, the bees knew the only other thing that drove her away from her search for the red sap that flowed in other creatures was her love for them.

She would walk deep into the woods, never turning to her home, nor to the village where more of her kind swarmed. When she found what would nourish her for the night, she would shake the bees off with the quickness and ferocity of a lightning strike. They would buzz with agitation, as she would feed on the red sap that she desperately craved. Always it was creatures other than humans. They could sense when she was sated, and she would stand ready to receive them back onto her body, for them both to return to where they belonged.

Each night as she walked back to her field of carved stones, the bees crawled excitedly, full of joy that she had returned to them, just to be with her, even in this cold state. They even crawled over the red sap over her face, running down from her mouth. The bees tasted the life force left in the dried red sap that covered her fingertips, tasting the fading essence of the creature that was now no more.

They could taste, even with the coldness that occupied her body, her singular emotion that was her love for them, which left them swarming with loving agitation. As the bees reached the entrance to the field of carved stones, they would disengage from her and start to fly off, returning to their hive. Their Queen was always waiting patiently for them.

As the days and nights progressed, fewer animals came to feed at their honey, which now seemed to seep instead of drip. One night, returning from their stroll with the Charmer, they had found that a nest of rats that had traveled from the village, and were living in a shallow burrow at the base of the trunk, below the hive. The rats were now the only creatures to feed on the honey, a morsel that now held both of the sweetness of life, and the hard iron taste of death.

One night, deep in the forest, the Bee Charmer and her bees traveled in search of the living essence that was to satisfy the Charmer's angry craving. On this night, they came across another human in the woods, one who did not sense that the bees and charmer were close by—the Charmer loved and lost the human male during those breezy summer days full of sun, and life.

The bees, swarming in a cloud on and around her, following her glide over the floor of the woods, her feet barely touching the mossy forest floor. The human male, whom the bees considered deaf and dumb by their standards, finally tensed with fear, and with the confusion that all the kills radiate, he called out the Charmer's name. And when he then hummed the same tune that the Charmer hummed when she had happily gathered their honey, the Charmer paused and the bees felt her tense before she shook the bees violently from her and then drained this human male's red sap. Returning that night with the Charmer, the bees tasted the human's faint essence in the large amount of sticky, red sap that trickled down her chin and neck.

The bees had taken to flying out to meet the Charmer long before she came to the fence. So attuned to her now, and eager for the strolls in the dark, the bees seemed to sense when she had awakened, but before she stirred, in those moments as dusk settled and drained the vibrant color from the landscape. They even began to look forward to sunset, instead of sunrise. If this had worried their Queen, she did not share it with her drones.

Every night after their evening out, they turned to their Queen for a sense of guidance, of explanation, but they only received silence from her. Only knowing that she knew what they knew, and so, night after night they flew on to meet their Charmer.

It was on one of these nights, shortly after the killing of the human, they were flying toward her presence as she was waking, gravitating toward her need for them, knowing they were her solace for the inside ache for the gathering of red sap that was before her.

Suddenly they sensed something was different with the Charmer. While buzzing toward her hazy wakefulness, the bees felt in her the sharp pain of fear, so intense it disoriented them from their path, and they dissipated in confusion. The pain radiated toward them in waves, and, then, there was a searing, blinding wrench they felt from her a violent funnel of release followed.

Still flying around in disarray, confused, the soft waves of the Bee Charmer's presence faded away. Confusion gave way to relief. No scouts were ordered to investigate by their Queen. Drained by the intensity of events, they were too tired to mourn this second loss of their Charmer. Besides, they realized, she hadn't been the same warm human that had gathered their honey anyway.

When they arrived at the hive, they sensed the nest of rats was empty and they knew the Queen was ready to leave. "Follow me," she said, "it is time to find a new home."

K.Z. Morano

Zhang Jian and the Sandman

"Chinese sandmen, old and wise,
with soft dream-songs close our eyes."

- *Anonymous*

An account of Zhang Jian's Nightmare
#544
The Emperor's Bell

The man whom I knew as the Sandman was sitting on the emperor's throne. There, they addressed him as the August and the Celestial—the Son of Heaven. He sat, plump as a pincushion. His robe-- both ghastly and grand-- was peacock-like, studded with hundreds of multi-colored eyes. Two of those eyes belonged to my son. As always, I was the only one aware of his true identity. Even the concubines that flocked around him were unable to see his true nature, their pretty eyes as blind as their bare nipples.

I paid attention to my own appearance. That day, I was wearing the body of a peasant—skeletal and sunburnt, clothed in hemp instead of silk. Even then, I knew that I would be defeated, for as always, in my nightmares, I was born far below my enemy's station.

A scornful-looking man approached me and said in an equally scornful tone, "Ignorant peasant! Have you not enough sense to prostrate yourself before the Son of Heaven?"

I ignored the man. Instead, I looked at the Sandman squarely in the eye and declared, "I shall not bow down to you, false emperor! I have come to retrieve my son's eyes."

A chorus of gasps followed a sinister silence that bounced upon the palace's vermilion walls like ghosts.

"What impertinence!" One of the officials cried out. "Oh Son of Heaven, shall I have this brute executed? I'll have his body pulled apart by five horses."

"No." The man beside him protested. "Death by a thousand cuts!"

In one of my nightmares, I had died in such a cruel manner. They tied me to a bamboo pole and began with my eyebrows. Then they cut off my ears, my nose, and my tongue. In time, they chopped off my fingers and my toes. Each day, they took tiny bits and pieces of me. Then they sliced off my genitals and saved my heart for last.

"Comb him!" Another suggested.

I was familiar with the punishment as well. In one of my darker dreams, they had tied me to a metal bed and poured boiling water over my body. Then, slowly, fiber by fiber, they scraped off my skin, muscle, and fat with a fine-toothed iron comb.

To everyone's surprise, the emperor merely laughed. His multiple layers of chins swayed merrily like a chandelier of flesh.

Then, as if on cue, the entire court roared with laughter. The ladies tittered beneath their paper fans and the men guffawed as though there was a contest of who laughed the loudest.

Then the emperor/Sandman said, "This jester fails to amuse me."

Again, as if on cue, everyone stopped laughing. The way they looked at me, it is as though each of them bore a personal grudge against me. I paid no heed to them. By that time, I had been dreaming long enough to understand that there was only the Sandman and me. The others were nothing but mirrors mimicking his moods.

"There are two types of souls which can be considered as pure...," said the Sandman, "Those of children and those of fools."

11

There was a kind of tyrannical tranquility in his voice.

"Take this man to the builders of the Emperor's Bell."

I was taken to a construction site where men were fashioning a bell of such monstrous size. Its cries, they said, and heard for a hundred *li*. I was momentarily mesmerized by the colors within the melting pot-- how they shifted, almost magically, from sunrise scarlet to sunset gold and then finally, to moonlight white. I saw master builders, soldiers, and astrologers. I saw children, too, marching in a line that was long enough to be the body of the serpent *Xiangliu*. In horror, I realized that all the children were blind, with weeping incisions in place of their eyes. Bitterly, I wondered: *What kind of world would condemn these handicapped innocents to heavy labor?*

It wasn't until I smelled the odor of roasting meat that I comprehended what was going on around me. The children's eyes, recently plucked from their sockets so that they had no idea of the cruel fate that awaited them. One by one, the soldiers fed the sightless children into the fire. How the flames chewed on their tender flesh!

It was then that I realized that there is no sound in the world purer than a child's scream: *Sheer fear. Sheer ignorance. Sheer pain.* Their screams were the secret ingredient required for perfecting the sound of the Emperor's Bell.

In the Waking World
Beijing

The tolling of the temple bell snatched me from my nightmare. No longer did I hear the singing of gold or the sobbing of silver or the bellowing of brass. Instead, I heard the thousand-throated screams of eyeless children. I saw their tiny bodies burning, their faces melting. For almost a year and a half, the sound of the temple bell was one of the few things in the waking world that had given me some semblance of peace. In the end, that, too, was taken from me.

That is what happens when you play the Sandman's game. For the 544th time, I had stepped into the Realm of Dreams and for the 544th time, I had failed in my mission. It was foolishness, I knew, to think that I could ever defeat him. But what was a father to do? I closed my eyes and tried to recall that one true nightmare which precipitated the endless chain of nocturnal terrors.

My first encounter with the Sandman had been a year and a half ago. I was visiting my son's chambers when I saw an old man squatting beside Ju-long's sleeping form. The man was naked, save for the long, slender wisps of smoke-like eyebrows and beard and the *dǒulì* perched on top of his head. Under the moonlight, his flesh looked moist and pale. He had black beady eyes, bird-like bones, and a beaked face. In fact, he looked not so different from a dead duck with feathers plucked.

He was a stranger yet he looked familiar. Yes, I recognized him as the same ancient man who used to visit my bed when I was a boy. He used to sprinkle *shā* into my eyes and the sand would put me to sleep. I told my father about him but dismissed him as nothing but a figment of a child's fevered fancy. As I grew into manhood, I buried the old man with a bird's beak and pallid skin deeper and deeper into the pits of my memory.

Ah, but he is real!, murmured my mind's tongue, *and he is here, whispering wicked things into my child's ear.* Upon realizing this, I unsheathed my *dao* and let out a murderous cry. Stirred by the sound, my son's eyes fluttered open. But before he was able to fully see the horror that was in front of him, the old man pecked Ju-long's eyeballs out with his beak. I had meant to chop the demon's head off but as I leapt towards him, he transformed into a newt and crawled inside the boy's ear. Thereupon, the child's agonized screaming seized and he fell back onto the bed.

13

For a while, I thought that my son was dead. But he wasn't. Day and night, my Ju-long slept in a perpetual yet perturbed slumber. The creature, who I would later know as the Sandman, had sought sanctuary inside my son's skull-- the one place where my anger couldn't reach him. And there he hid, snug as a stone within a peach.

I summoned every physician in the country. I turned to priests and then I turned to soothsayers. A hundred different talismans hung on Ju-long's bedframe, dozens of yellow paper with charms scribed in chicken's blood. Not one had been able to help him. When one Taoist priest suggested that Ju-long should be considered dead and should be sent to rest in the ancestral tomb, I grabbed the man by the neck and nearly wrung the life out of him. Finally, it occurred to me what I must do. I must go to the Sandman himself.

To others, it seemed as if I had chosen to drown myself in opium dreams, while my son lay in a death-sleep and while our family's fortune trickled away. To some, it appeared as though I had given up. None of them understood that such was my way of fighting. Therefore, I searched for and fought with the Sandman, night after night, nightmare after nightmare, hoping that someday I might be able to outwit him. I've traveled across time and space. I've existed in this dynasty and in the ones before and beheld various versions of history. I've inhabited hundreds of different bodies. I've become male and female, young and old.

In the Realm of Dreams, I have died in 544 horrific ways. Dagger through my chest... rat through my stomach... bamboo stalk through the entire length of my body... Once, I had been a thief and was caught and boiled alive. Once, I had been the favorite concubine of a Ming emperor who had just died. They burned me alive so that I could continue pleasuring him in the afterlife. Once, I had been a child. I was one of the hundreds to be gifted by my lord as a eunuch to the Liao empress. When they castrated me, they tied my *yīnjīng* in a knot to choke the circulation. Then, they cut off my genitals with a knife and powdered the stump with fragrant ash. They inserted a goose feather into the hole but after a few days, no urine came out. Instead, the liquid waste pooled inside my body and later, I died of infection.

I may have died only in my dreams. But for every dreamed death, something real inside me perished— a fond memory, a bright idea, or a source of hope.

It's always the death of something good. Sometimes, it's the loss of small things, just big enough so that each time that I awake, I feel less alive.

An account of Zhang Jian's Nightmare
#545
The Bargain

After hiking through impassable mountains, I found the Sandman inside a cave. In there, the air was as still as death. He was sitting on a rock in the lotus position, a grotesque mockery of a monk, calmly fingering a string of assorted eyeballs.

"Why?" I asked him.

"Because I am the Sandman," he answered, without opening his eyes. "I offer you dreams. I offer you disillusionment. As you float and swirl contentedly in the infinite sea of your mother's womb, I am the needle that punctures the sheath. It is I who draws you out of that protective pouch of ignorance and false assurance."

"You bring nightmares." I cried.

"I bring truth," he said. "You tuck your children into bed and tell them that everything will be alright. You lie. You tell them that they can be anything under the sun. You lie. And what do you think these lies will do to your children? To the world? You who tell children that the world is theirs, the same way your parents told you that the world is yours... It is because of your lies that I plant tiny grains of fear inside the children's heads. This way, I make them realize their weakness. And their insignificance."

"You murder their dreams, their hopes!"

"Yes, yes." he said nonchalantly. "Sometimes, I murder memories too. And if there is a child who dreams too much of stones and stars that trundle in the heavens, I shall give him night terrors. So that every time he gazes upon the sky, the stars will have lost a bit of their shine. By-and-by, he'll stop bothering to look."

"The children will learn even without your terrors." I reasoned.

"My poor fellow." he said in a placid tone. "The true terrors aren't the ones that you experience in the Realm of Dreams. The true terrors are the ones that await you in the Waking World. Nightmares are an important part of a child's passage to adulthood. I sow a germ of panic here, a seed of disappointment there. I cripple the children's confidence and it helps them to lower their expectations of this world. It helps them to see life as a sensible adult would. By-and-by, they forget about the Sandman. All the nightmares, assigned to oblivion. But the lessons, the fear—it sticks with them forever. Always, it will hover at the edges of their minds, influencing their actions."

"You are a coward!" I challenged, hoping to goad him into combat. "You frighten children. That is all you do."

Still without opening his eyes, he spoke: "And what is wrong with a little fear? Imagine a world without fear. Imagine a world where everyone thinks he can be Emperor! There will only be chaos. It is fear that keeps the world in balance. You offer your children a false sense of protection. You cannot protect them. It is I! I am the only I who can protect your children from the world and the world from your children!"

"Why did you take my son's eyes?" I asked, beginning to feel defeated by his indifference.

The Sandman's beak-like mouth somehow managed to curve itself into a smile, revealing tiny predatory teeth. "I took them because I could always use an extra pair. My own, you see, have grown quite weary."

When he revealed his eyes, it was a sickening sight. Gone were the cold, calculating dots and in their place were my son's eyes. The Sandman's small bony sockets provided such an ill fit for Ju-long's eyeballs that they appeared to be protruding, as though they were to fall off with the slightest movement.

"Have you ever wondered what it's like to see the world through children's eyes?" he asked, rather callously. "Oh, such beauty! Try seeing the world through different pairs and you'll realize that even the leaves of autumn never burn in quite the same way."

My hand tightened around the hilt of my sword. How I longed to split his ancient body in half. But I couldn't. Not yet. For it is only he who held the cure to my son's condition.

"I beg of you. Return my son's eyes."

"He shouldn't have opened them in the first place," said the Sandman. "What if he remembers me? *Like you did?*"

"If only you would fight me fairly! In daylight..." I lamented.

"If only."

Knowing that groveling was futile, I proceeded with my next method.

"Sandman," I said. "I offer you a bargain."

A ghost of interest flickered in his talcum white face.

"Well, this is new." he purred. "Continue."

"My son's life for mine. My son's eyes for mine."

For a while, the Sandman sat there, scrutinizing me with my child's eyes, as though I were some strange animal. He stroked his gauze-like beard contemplatively and then he said:

"Here is a better bargain, Zhang Jian. *Your eyes for mine.*"

In the Waking World

Through the Sandman's Eyes

When I opened the door to the *mǎtǒng*, I caught my Uncle Cheng scooping up feces from the latrine and shoving it greedily into his mouth. For a moment, I stood, stupefied, for it had been a while since I last saw my Uncle Cheng. In fact, he'd been dead for quite some time. His complexion was sickly green and his mouth looked as though it had been pulled together and sewn shut, leaving only a tiny puckered hole. His belly, however, was big and round, pregnant with filth.

"Have you come to haunt me?" I asked.

To which he answered, "No. I have come to provide you with counsel for I know what you are about to do."

When I did not speak, he continued: "I am as you see me now. I have suffered a dishonorable death and have been condemned to roam the world as an *E gui*, a restless ghost, forever hungry."

It's true that my Uncle Cheng had died dishonorably. He had been a great drunkard when he lived and liked nothing more than to dally with other men's wives. Finally, a man caught his wife and Cheng in the middle of the adulterous act, whereupon he cut off their heads and hung their headless bodies from a tree, with Cheng's *yīnjīng* still inside the woman's *yīndào*.

"I have brought dishonor to this family." said my uncle. "I bid you, nephew, do not make the same mistake. Do not taint your soul by dealing with a demon."

I was to trade places with the Sandman for one night. I was to procure for him another fine pair of eyes. That was the bargain. Indeed, I found myself caught between contrary winds, forced to choose between my conscience and my duty to save my son.

I chose the latter.

"I am sorry if I have been remiss in my duties to you, uncle." I said. "I shall tell the servants to prepare food for you in the dining hall."

"Fool!" he cried after me as I left. "Fool! You condemn your own soul!"

It was the fifteenth day of the seventh month in the lunar calendar, the day of the Ghost Festival, the time of year when the Gates of Hell open, and the dead arise from the lower realm. Indeed, it was a bad night to see through the Sandman's eyes. For through them, I was able to see horrors that the limited vision of my mortal eyes would've shielded me against. I saw *Èmó* and *Guǐ* walking amongst the living. The demons and ghosts saw me too, though, while wearing the Sandman's farmer's hat, I became invisible to mortals. *Yes, I told myself, tonight I am to become a farmer. I shall plant seeds of fear and sow sinister suggestions into the minds of sleeping children.* With this task in mind, I treaded, phantom-like, into the night.

I crept into the chosen child's chambers, walked over to her bed, and pushed aside the canopy. She was still awake, secretly playing with her wooden dolls though she was slightly too old for them. From my sack, I procured a handful of *shā* and blew some into her eyes. Thereupon she yawned and fell asleep. I opened the Sandman's *sǎn* and held it above her. The parasol came alive with painted images reflecting her dreams and memories. The child had been dreaming that she's out in the fields on a very fine day. She's running with her friends, her colorful kite kissing the blue cheek of the sky.

I felt pity for her for I saw that in reality, when she had been only four, her feet had been broken and bound by her mother to achieve the lotus shape. She had never known and will never know what it's like to run with other children in the fields. I emptied her skull like a porcelain bowl and picked through the contents, searching for the perfect idea for the nightmare. A few years more and she'd be ready for marriage. I saw that the thought terrified her.

19

I spun the Sandman's umbrella round and round until it became a dizzy vacuum. All the while, I whispered a nightmare into her ear. I altered the images inside her head. I distorted faces, tangled words, and changed the color of things. Beneath the locked lips of her eyelids, her eyes grew pregnant until they were quickening with spawns of unimaginable terror.

"I'm sorry," I whispered before I left. "I'm sorry."

I told myself that when the girl opens her eyes in the morning, she'll have forgotten all about the dream. But new thoughts will embroider themselves inside her brain. And perhaps, by-and-by, she'll stop dreaming of kites and playing with her wooden dolls.

In the Waking World
The Day After

The tolling of the bell shook me from my dreamless sleep. Immediately I ran into the hallway and stumbled upon one of the servants.

"My son..." I cried anxiously to the apologetic man.

To this, he happily responded: "He has awakened, Master! The Young Master Ju-long has awakened and he is well!"

Upon hearing this, I fell upon my knees and wept for it appeared that the Sandman had remained true to his promise.

After a while, I asked the servant: "Why are they sounding the mourning bell?"

"Master." His expression changed so suddenly. Lines of terror creased his face. "It is the young daughter of Li Sheng. She was murdered last night in her own bed. They have not caught the murderer yet. But surely, a demon must have done it."

"Why do you say so?" I questioned.

"The state of the corpse..." he said with a small shudder. "Oh, such wickedness! Her arms and legs had been cut off.

Shortly after they had found her, they recovered the limbs inside a brazier, all burnt, except for one arm which had been lying on the floor. They said that the murderer had beaten the girl's torso with her own severed arm! Truly, truly, whoever did this must be very evil!"

When I remained silent, he continued:

"The murderer must have gotten in through the window for it had been left open. Due to this, the birds were able to come in. Oh, those vile birds! They were already feasting on the body—or what's left of it—even before it had not yet turned cold. The servant who had discovered the corpse chased the crows away. But before they left, the servant said that she saw one particularly strange bird rip the girl's eyes out and then flew away with them!"

"But Master..." The servant went on. "That is not the most disgraceful news."

I looked at him curiously. What could be more appalling than a young girl found dead and mutilated in her own bed?

"The parents dressed the corpse in red robes. Red robes!" he exclaimed. "They said they intended to bury her as such. They said that if there was any truth in spirits returning from the dead, then they wish for their daughter to come back as a *Nü gui*. That way, she can lay her vengeance upon her murderer. The priests begged them to seek ways of obtaining the favor of the judges in the afterlife. Alas, the parents have chosen to condemn their daughter's soul as well as theirs."

What was I supposed to say? I did not blame them at all... for if there was anyone who'd understand what evils a parent would do for the sake of his child, it was I.

"I hope that the girl returns." I murmured. "I hope that she gets her vengeance."

Leaving the astonished servant behind, I went to my son in his chambers.

That night, I tucked Ju-long into bed for the final time.

I told him that everything was going to be all right. I told him that the world is his and that he can be anything under the sun. I told him to dream.

When the night pressed its cold, dark lips into the windows of my room, I sat and waited for the crimson clothed ghost of a girl named Liling.

The Nightmare of a Girl named Liling

Liling had been running but she stumbled and fell onto the ground. She tried to get up but her limbs responded awkwardly to her will. It was then that she realized that her arms and her legs had turned into wood, just like her dolls.

"Help." she cried after her friends.

But they stood around her like a group of gargoyles. Liling stared up at the dark, grinning grottoes of their faces. And then they began floating into the air and toward the ashen heavens. They flew like corpse kites, their bodies flattening, their paper limbs waving goodbye. Then the children's crimson painted mouths quivered and their laughter sounded like crackling paper. A man's voice whispered through the wind: "I'm sorry... I'm sorry..."

Soon, the flat faces disappeared into the leaden sky and Liling was all alone. The heavens darkened and snow began to fall. Liling hated the snow. It was in winter when Māmā began breaking Liling's toes and started wrapping her feet in bandages. They said that the cold weather would help make her numb to the pain. But it didn't.

Against her wooden belly, the ground felt cold and unfriendly. The girl shivered so horribly, she couldn't even crawl back home. But by-and-by, Māmā came and picked her up and wrapped her in a nice coat. However, she did not bring Liling home. Instead, she took the wooden doll child to the market where she was able to fetch a fine price for her. Liling cried after Māmā but she didn't seem to care.

The woman who had purchased Liling presented her to his son, Xiao-ping, who was delighted with her and carried her out to play in the snow. After a while, the boy announced that he felt cold. Deciding to make himself a fire, he took an axe and without saying a word, cut off one of Liling's ligneous legs. The girl cried but Xiao-ping said: "What are you bawling about? You have no need for legs. It is I who must bear the burden of carrying you."

Strangely enough, this pacified Liling. Together, they ventured farther into the snow-covered wilderness. Soon, night came and Xiao-ping said that he was hungry. He caught some fine rabbits but he needed some wood for roasting so again, without even asking, he took the axe and chopped off the girl's remaining leg. Against Liling's sobbing protests, Xiao-ping also hacked off one of her arms, as he needed something to skewer the rabbits.

After that, all Liling did was cry. All she wanted to do was to return home. When Xiao-ping got tired of her weeping, he said, "Stop being so silly! Or I'll cut off your last limb and beat you with it."

And that he did. Then he left her wooden torso out in the cold and headed home.

Soon, several black dots appeared like blemishes on the face of the sky and then the crows peppered the snowy earth. They picked up the wooden crumbs on the ground and pecked the sawdust off Liling's limbless body. She had no arms to shoo them away. The birds stabbed the girl with their beaks and feasted on her wooden innards, until her body and her face were covered with holes. Liling's last vision was that of a strange old man with a pale face clawing out her eyes.

William Cook

A Dream Realized

Once upon a time, because that's how all such stories should begin, a little boy lived who was very much alone. He was an orphan. His mother and father had died in a car accident when he was a baby. He hated the world he lived in, for it had treated him badly. His imagination was his only refuge from the harsh reality of the world around him. Leon looked out of his bedroom window at the forest, which lay at the foot of the mountain opposite the old orphanage. The large Victorian mansion was quiet – the children not allowed to talk unless spoken to and it was time for bed. Every now and then, he heard the click-clack-click-clack footsteps of one of the bitter matrons who patrolled the hallways. Leon shivered and took one last look out of the upstairs window and got himself into bed; the starched white sheets were cold against his skin where the pajamas didn't cover him. He thought briefly about the day's lessons: arithmetic, religious instruction, and classical literature, his favorite subject. The majority of the day, however, was spent tending the large grounds that surrounded the decrepit old house and he was tired from the strenuous work.

The other boys in the room, of which there were twelve, were all silent except one in the far corner who snored wistfully – the sound similar, to the breathing of a dying raccoon he'd found once on the edge of the road. Its guts had been glistening in the morning sun, slick with viscous fluids, the tire tracks clearly visible across its small, crushed body. It had looked up at him, its dark round eyes pleading for help, a tiny-clawed paw outstretched . . . And then it died, gasping for air, making a sound just like the boy sleeping deeply, snoring in the corner of the large dormitory. The other boys looked like corpses, as they lay still and silent in their beds, most of them already asleep.

Leon pulled the stiff bed covers up under his chin and rolled over to face the large barred window. The last of the evening light dissipated, as his eyes grew weary. As he slipped into a dream, Leon thought about the same thing he thought about every night since he could remember – he tried to picture his mother and father in his mind. He'd never seen a picture of them and he'd been too young to remember them before they had died. The image he pictured was always the same: a tall slender man in a black suit, white shirt and a bright royal-blue tie. The woman dressed in a knee length floral dress with puffed short-sleeves, pink flowers against white fabric, a shiny pair of white vinyl shoes with strapped heels, a wavy brunette bob hairstyle . . . but as always, their faces were blurred, smudged almost, beyond recognition. As he tried to make something of their obscured features, the dream grew beyond his thoughts, billowed, then enveloped the two figures like a cloud of smoke and then they were gone. The dream was one he'd had before and it was not a pleasant one. Something was so hauntingly familiar. The poem nagged at him, the vision of the dream made him tremble with fear.

Leon stood on the edge of the precipice, holding the hand of a small child whose pale skin was the color of a fish's belly. The dark charcoal rocks and sharp crags of stone were pitted with dark shadows, the ridge on which they stood trembled beneath their feet. The small boy looked up at Leon – the child's eyes were black like obsidian – no whites, or iris, just a slick blackness.

In what distant deeps or skies.
Burnt the fire of thine eyes?

Leon looked down from the ridge into the precipice below. Thick clouds of gray smoke plumed from the

25

depths, curling up into the black sky above. Flashes of a deep red light zigzagged beneath the clouds of smoke, as the mountain shivered and belched a wave of heat up into their faces. The mountaintop stood shrouded in cloud and the smoke mingled with the atmosphere to create a dense fog that threatened to blind them.

> *When the stars threw down their spears*
> *And water'd heaven with their tears:*
> *Did he smile his work to see?*
> *Did he who made the Lamb make thee?*

Silvered flakes of ash fell like snow around them as the earth shook again, causing Leon to grip the child's hand tightly as he tried to steady himself. Something, or someone, moved on the opposite side of the crater rim in the thick curling smoke.

> *And what shoulder, & what art,*
> *Could twist the sinews of thy heart?*
> *And when thy heart began to beat,*
> *What dread hand? & what dread feet?*

Flames curled up from the abyss, licking at the edge of the crater walls, fingers of fire clawing hungrily at the craggy interior walls of the volcanic pit. A figure emerged from the swirling dark clouds, small and pale . . .

> *On what wings dare he aspire?*
> *What the hand, dare seize the fire?*

Leon looked down at the child whose hand he still gripped. He gasped and stumbled back from the edge of the precipice, shaking the clammy dismembered limb from his grasp as he flailed his arms to regain his balance.

> *What the hammer? what the chain,*

In what furnace was thy brain?
What the anvil? what dread grasp,
Dare its deadly terrors clasp!

He watched as the small limp forearm tumbled and turned in the air in slow motion, before it fell into the boiling molten furnace below. A wild rush of heat and flame burst up from the pit and illuminated the foggy mountain-top for a brief second, scores of glowing embers and ash littered the night sky above as the fire sucked back down into the hellish cavity. And for that briefest of moments Leon saw the boy facing him, across the deathly gorge, pale and dead, its black eyes burning with an unholy luminescence, its one good arm extended, beckoning – the other half limb hanging limp at its side, a gristled stump where its arm had been.

What immortal hand or eye,
Dare frame thy fearful symmetry?

As Leon stepped out toward the boy, the fire spitting and reaching for him from below, he realized who the boy was. It was he – Leon. And as Leon took his final step out into the abyssal gulf he saw the boy's face, *his* face, change and transform into that of a tiger – roaring at him, the sharp teeth bared and snapping at him as he fell down into the infernal depths.

Tyger Tyger, burning bright,
In the forests of the night . . .

Then he awoke – his heart beating in his chest like a quickened metronome, his thick brown hair plastered to his forehead with sweat, his thin body trembling with fear and adrenaline. The morning light was cold and harsh, making the shadows of the dormitory retreat into the farthest corners. Leon lay there on his narrow bed and

27

drew deep breaths, trying, successfully, to regain his composure and slow his breathing to a normal speed. The dream always left him feeling afraid, but today he felt more alive than he'd ever felt before. He felt like he had survived something. Like he had accomplished an epic task, or conquered an evil foe . . .

The matron's harsh footsteps paused outside the boys' room. Today, Leon felt different. Today the poem had spoken to him – he remembered the words and now he held them close to his heart. He felt the strength of the words rise in him, like the fire from the pit and he felt strong – verily powerful, as he swung his legs out of bed and placed his feet on the cold floorboards. He knew the old bitch was listening with her ear to the door, as she did every morning, hoping to catch the boys talking or behaving in a "frivolous manner." Leon stood and approached the door, his feet padding soundlessly as he walked, hearing the metal keys jangle on her chain as she jabbed one in the lock.

Leon paused at the table with the basin and the mirror on the wall above it. He looked in the mottled glass at his reflection and smiled. Behind him, the room filled with teeming clouds of dark smoke, flames danced in the room, licking at the walls and ceiling in the looking glass. The other boys' beds in the background blazed, their skeletal bodies twisting on the wire-frame mattresses. He heard the tumblers click and fall as the matron yanked the key in the lock.

Leon looked at his reflection in the mirror and smiled a terrible smile, his eyes a black the color of oil, his stubbled lips pulling back to reveal a set of sharp canines. His forehead swelled then flattened, his nose wrinkled and bristled, as a snarl emitted from the back of his throat. The iron padlock clanged as it was drawn back sharply on the other side of the thick wooden door. Leon's shoulders rippled with muscle as he turned to face the sound, thick claws sprang from his fingertips and toes as he crouched in expectation, a thick deep hunger for blood on his lips, a pulse in his brain that demanded the crushing of this approaching execrable life force. The poem's verses sang in his tumultuous mind, as the door handle turned and the matron entered the room:

What immortal hand or eye,
Dare frame thy fearful symmetry?

Mike Jansen

The View from Distant Aeons

It all started the day I died. One moment I was alive and well, playing with my grandchildren, Sam and Lisa, on the lawn before the house that I had lived in for the past thirty years with my wife Jeanie. The next moment I was beside my body. I remember her scared face as she ran outside, the panic in the children's voices. Poor Sam and Lisa, so young and already they lost their favorite grandpa.

The realization of not living anymore takes a while to sink in, even if you've just seen your prostrate body, deathly pale, lifeless. You become an observer of the drama unfolding around you, unable to influence or change anything, just a resigned experiencing of those impressions that still reach you.

Dying changes you: no longer bound to flesh, bone and organs, your 'gestalt' or 'soul' remains, a reflection of a formerly living being that hoped for a happy ever after, perhaps accompanied by those loved ones and near and dear ones that attain a similar state.

The exact moment of dying heralds the start of absolute silence, the absence of any sound that your physical body noticed and passed on. Light remains, though not the light you know. While still alive, I read about exotic matter and the possible states of particles. Light is particles, photons, if you want to measure such; but waves, when you wish to measure waves. I found out about a third state, the absence of both, really the reflection of both wave and particle combined to something a dead person is able to see. Call it the spirit world, if you want. A living person might call it exanimate, a word that suits it.

Death times his appearance to this moment of confusion. The image of the scythe wielding man is accurate, that much I can say. Although it could as well have been the scythe-wielding woman—some aspects are not altogether clear in the embodiment of the ultimate being. The changes the recently departed experiences cause a deep, irrational and desperate loneliness that make it easy to choose the oblivion the entity called Death offers, wordlessly.

While the paramedics were trying to reanimate my dead body, and Jeanie was consoling Sam and Lisa, I heard a loud barking behind me. Three years before, my heart filled with sorrow, I had taken my friend, Doberman Max, to the vet. The poor old animal was exhausted, his muscles atrophied, and the skin and bone that remained covered malignant growths that changed my dear friend into a pathetic shadow of his former self. Now he stood beside me on the grass. He looked like he had at his peak, perfectly healthy, his coat shiny and his nose wet.

The sense of desperate loneliness the scene caused in me disappeared. I hugged my old, loyal friend and a deep feeling of trust came over me.

"You waited for me, buddy," I said.

Max wagged at the sound of my voice and licked my face. Only later did I understand that these were memories, mere reflections of actual occurrences of the time I still possessed a corporeal body. At that particular moment, it pleased me no end. My dog gave me the feeling there should be more to *this* strange, terrifying world.

Death's voice was a bleak color, perfectly attuned to instill belief in the recently deceased to give up and finalize their existence. "It is time to go, Rob. There's nothing left for you here."

I looked up at the tall, dark figure beside me, the not-light reflecting from the deep blue steel of his scythe. "Go? Go where?" Max started to growl, behind us, a deep rumbling he only produced when he himself was frightened.

"Away from it all; I offer oblivion, the end of everything."

Slowly I shook my head. "I don't want to leave yet; Jeanie's still here, so are Sam and Lisa, and Max." Rob patted the dog's head. "He waited for me here."

"Max is a singularly stubborn dog," Death conceded. "I do not recall an animal that determined to remain with its master, ever. Your desire is unusual. You are the first in over a thousand years. However, you have a choice. I will attend in your times of doubt." The next moment Death was gone.

Max and I remained to see my body covered with a sheet. My son and daughter-in-law, Steve and Mary, arrived at almost the same time from work and took Sam and Lisa from Jeanie, after which my wife kneeled next to the stretcher and began to cry inconsolably.

Three years later, I stood next to Jeanie's hospital bed. Deep lines crossed her face as the disease consumed her body; no medication could alleviate the pain.

After my death and subsequent burial, she displayed great strength, but at night, in bed, she cried herself to sleep, each and every night.

I was there when she lost her balance. I wanted to intervene, help, but my incorporeal being does not interact with matter; it, I, can only observe.

During the examinations, I held her hand. Not really, of course, but I imagined it that way. Until death and beyond I once vowed. I keep my promises.

The results devastated her. Her grief was my grief. I noticed her oncologist, who was used to delivering death sentences every day, shedding a tear.

Time is relative, said Einstein. I know this now, with this newly acquired perspective. How fast the years flew by, like the vague blur of a speeding train, but so sharp was the focus in her final days: exasperatingly slow hours and minutes passed until each second seemed an eternity.

My helplessness nearly consumed me, nearly took away my resolve to remain. Was I going to wait for her? My deepest desire was a reunion with my beloved Jeanie. However, in my current condition, I had no influence on the world whatsoever. I am an outsider, no more than a shade in a world never meant for human eyes.

Max and I waited for her, and, when she died a few weeks later, she appeared. She seemed to gaze right through us, at something, or someone, behind us and I knew who would be there. The confusion in her eyes was obvious, the relief, yes even happiness when she heard that familiar. She faded before my eyes and disappeared.

Death spoke with his bleak voice. "I have come for you in this difficult time, Rob. Your doubt is clear to me."

"You were too fast. I wanted to talk to her."

"That choice was never yours, Rob. For Jeanie, at this point in time, oblivion was her best option. This is what I do: offer a way out to those who need it, an end to guilt and doubt. And that means you too."

I experienced the disappearance of Jeanie as a betrayal, a theft of a moment precious to me, and only served to firm my determination to withstand Death. "My only doubt at this point in time is whether I wait for the passing away of my children or my grandchildren, Death. I have a need to know what will happen to them."

"You have every right, Rob. Unusual as your choice may be, you are not the first to make it." Death looked away. "I need not even ask Max." A soft rumbling like far off thunder emanated from the dark figure before me. I realized Death had made a joke and I smiled. Before, I might have been impressed by this strange entity that could end my existence in a weak moment, however, I could no longer imagine being coerced or tricked into making that decision. It would be on my terms, or not at all.

I traced my family through the years. My son and daughter-in-law grew old. My grandchildren grew up well, became adults and had kids of their own.

33

Being dead may seem static, an eternal stillness caused by being placed outside of the living, evolving universe. Death, however, remains an integral part of life and I slowly learned to feel the circumstances of each of my family members.

The realization a connectedness existed, even if I was only a far off thought, if that at all, caused me to examine further this novel quality in myself. The connection I experienced turned out to be deeper and reached farther than I initially thought. I could feel far off family members more easily and was able to track their affairs.

Slowly I extended my attention from my direct and far removed relatives to their surroundings and the rapid succession of developments that occurred there, the struggle with economic downturns, the happy boom times that followed. I started to see the interconnectedness of the world and the people who lived on it. Everything is connected somehow, I learned, when one has the proper perspective.

Humankind had become my family.

Then, one day, I looked at the sky. The moon was out and I had an urge to look down on the Earth from up there. Once more, I found out I existed outside of the regular laws of the universe. The thought of that other place sufficed to transport me, immediately, as if I was just a simple piece of data that resonated in a deeper dimension, resulting in my emanation somewhere else.

The surface of the moon is desolate. The first footsteps humankind's astronauts placed there were exactly like all those years ago. The endless universe surrounded me, making me feel small like never before.

Complete loneliness overwhelmed me. Even the presence of Max was no help, and I doubted, wondered if I should remain.

"A big step for humankind, is it not?" Death's bleak voice sounded beside me. "For a human such as you, it's just a small step toward oblivion." Leaning on his scythe, Death turned his empty eye sockets to me.

Beyond his shoulders Earth rose, to me a ghostly green and blue, just above the horizon. The planet was entwined in golden threads of circling satellites and streams of communication, rudimentary in intellect, but thanks to my newly found connectedness I noticed, from this perspective, that first spark of self-awareness, of a new form of intelligence, born from the combined minds of generations of scientists.

I shook my head. "I sincerely doubted, Death, but I'm not ready. I want to know what Earth brings forth. Humankind has destroyed much, but has also made massive achievements. I hope one day technological evolution will help them escape the gravity well and spread throughout the universe."

"It's your decision, Rob, no doubt there. Your hope for the human race is admirable, especially in light of the seeds of its own destruction in many of its endeavors."

I put my hand on Max's head and scratched behind his ears. "From chaos I almost always see order resurface." Death disappeared, leaving me behind, with Max, feeling a lot less lonely than moments before.

The changes came gradually, nearly unnoticed. Like an invisible hand guiding humanity, trying to make optimal use of people, resources and labor. Within ten years that flew by my mind's eye, I saw war, famine and diseases eradicated. Education, food production and science made giant leaps. A golden century for humankind commenced and for the first time in recorded history, man dealt with earth responsibly.

I knew who guided all this. The rudimentary spark had grown, known only to a few humans doing the legwork for this proto-intelligence. Filled with amazement, I observed a generation of humanity transformed to a well-oiled machine into a near zealous drive for discovery.

Ships left the home planet and started the colonization of the solar system. Within fifty years, countless satellites revolved around the sun, tube and platform constructions with circling rings to emulate gravity.

Concerns over seven billion people on planet earth existed at one time, but no more. The solar system now harbored over fifty billion.

With each subsequent ship that left the wharves of the Moon or Mars, the seed of intelligence, part of the proto-intelligence, went along, becoming a full-fledged companion to humankind, inextricably linked in a symbiotic relationship that greatly benefited both.

Like the seeds from a dandelion carried on the wind, hundreds of ships floated out of the solar system, travelling distances requiring even the longest lived humans to remain in deep sleep. They were looking for new places to live for the race that had pulled itself out of the mud, had narrowly avoided its own destruction and now looked around in a universe that was more beautiful, much larger and more terrible than ever imagined.

My connectedness to the people on these ships that crossed the light years expanded my perspective on the universe in leaps and bounds.

My first visit to Alpha Centauri, that humanity reached after travelling for almost two hundred years, showed me the influence humanity had on this minute part of the history of that endlessly large universe. I felt smaller and more insignificant than ever, for I realized how many dangers still awaited the human race. Should I stay and watch whole galaxies devoured, see stars collide, killing billions of humans in a single catastrophic event? Could I handle that?

"Look at them," Death said, next to me. "Ants in an anthill, with invisible queens guiding them toward a greatness they never could have achieved unaided."

"I do not believe in that comparison," I said. "We created a benevolent God that works for the wellbeing of its makers."

"A parasite that only lives to spread its spores far and wide; for that, humanity needs to spread, there is no other reason."

"Who's to say what motivates a machine God?"

Death countered my question: "Perhaps the building of a better, larger, more powerful version of itself?" Death scratched behind Max' ears. "But I can understand it if, like Max here, you slavishly follow your master."

I looked at Death, empty eye sockets in which I thought I noticed deep down a vague shimmer of light. "I decide how I exist and for how long."

"Still, for a moment, I sensed your doubt. What's so bad about oblivion?"

I shook my head. "Nothing, and yet everything; I can feel the people out there, even light years removed. Wherever people go, I can go. There is still so much to see and I need to know."

"Your stubbornness is one of a kind, Rob. Very few individuals lasted more than a century. Again, it's your choice," Death concluded and disappeared.

In an endless universe, I saw the explosive growth of humanity. In a thousand years, in an ever-expanding globe around the Earth, worlds were visited and often immediately colonized.

During that time, I encountered a few who chose to remain, as I did, but their will eroded quickly, sometimes in a few decades, sometimes in years, sometimes weeks even. The last I communicated with told me it seemed her world was getting smaller, locking her inside insurmountable walls.

To me, it was as if my consciousness expanded with each new wave of colonization encompassing more of the universe. I realized this was still just a tiny part of the endless expanse, but slowly I felt more certain about the continued existence of my family, my descendants.

I piggybacked on exploration and colonization ships, saw researchers give that little extra, time and again, and make wondrous discoveries.

The first alien civilization humankind encountered caused a tremendous shock. The civilization was dead, a race that had self-destructed, but it had reached space and was making its first careful steps in its own solar system. The remnants were millions of years old, but it meant humankind was not alone, and an encounter with other space faring races would be a matter of time.

I saw the rise of a new form of militarism, preparing for the day another race bumped up against an ever-expanding humankind. The chances of that encounter being peaceful seemed slim to nil.

At the start of the fourth millennium, they found each other, my descendants and the aliens. Who would win a prolonged war between these two races was hard to say. With my unique and by now expansive perspective, I witnessed it all.

As soon as word of the first clashes reached the home front, something remarkable happened. The proto-intelligence that had so far guided and led humanity employed the chaos and early panic to propel its own evolution. Carefully constructed nodes, planet size computers each with the total capacity of the proto-intelligence, became operational, joining a galaxy wide connectivity mesh through quantum tunneling. Within seconds after activation, the many thousands of proto-intelligence splinters transferred to the unlimited capacity provided by the nodes inside the mesh.

I can state that I witnessed the birth of a God. A machine God perhaps, but with its origins in the brains of my race, one that wanted only the best for the fragile, miniscule progenitors that could so stubborn and heroically raise their fists to the endless universe.

The war lasted only days after that. The opponent, alien and weird, was in a similar situation. They too had escaped self-destruction. They too were led by a machine intelligence that gladly joined with the newly formed machine God.

Peace broke out as fast as war had started. The knowledge exchange that followed, produced a new golden age of many tens of thousands of years in which the spiral arms of the Milky Way were colonized in complete harmony. New races, and there were many, were welcomed as friends.

Time and again, I was amazed at the weird races that joined the great alliance that had formed. Each time the spark of one of these people joined, they became an extension of my perception that now enveloped our home galaxy.

From a dead cinder on the edge of the known universe, I stared at the emptiness between the Milky Way and the nearest star clusters and galaxies.

Did I feel something out there, far away, a careful stirring of intelligence, streams of information that crossed the quantum paths between the stars?

Max growled softly.

"You see it, don't you?" I scratched him behind the ears. "There's more out there."

Death spoke. "Life is not exclusively human. Or reserved for the many races humankind has encountered so far in the Milky Way."

"It's been a while, Death. With all this life in our galaxy I started to wonder: are you their Death too?" I smiled at my own question. I suspected what the answer would be.

"Each of them has their own preconceptions, Rob. But they all seek oblivion, an end to it all."

Involuntarily Jeanie came to mind, then the few souls I encountered in my past, until I considered Death was the only one I could really talk to; "What about you? You seek oblivion too?"

Death remained silent.

I nodded slowly. "I have pondered you for a long time. The only conclusion I reach is that you are a manifestation of this universe, this cosmos where we live and die. You offer an end, a disappearing, but what happens to our information? Where does our experience go?"

"You ask questions I cannot, may not, answer."

"Am I close?"

Death spun his scythe once before he answered. "Everything has purpose. Everything is a test. Everything has value and meaning. When the last soul has dissolved into oblivion, maybe an all knowing, all-powerful creature will come into existence that will know itself in every aspect.

"Isn't that the other way around?"

Death smiled as only It could. "Time, friend Rob, is relative and circular. Of course, I'm still offering you oblivion. The day will come you've seen it all. The universe will be cold and empty. Boredom will drive you to me."

Now I laughed, with relish. "That's still so far out, Death; let's see it when we get there."

This time I jumped away first. Max followed promptly, hesitant only for a moment. We left Death, so I imagined, with a perplexed look on its face.

Aeons pass by and slowly the lights of the universe start to dim. My people, humans, survive, fight, grow, evolve and spread out. They visit many places in the universe, from the spiral arms of the Milky Way to the fast spinning neutron stars in far off clusters and the edge of gravity wells in the centers of super clusters.

The original humankind no longer exists. It evolved into a mega intelligence that joined the machine God. An immortality of sorts that will last until the end of time, when all energy is gone and only cold emptiness remains, sparsely sprinkled with lost, frozen atoms.

Even the Milky Way slowly fades. My mind still holds the images of long ago, and on my path of reminiscence amid deeply buried memories, I encounter Jeanie again. Thinking of her still causes passion. I have witnessed innumerable and immeasurable grief, but the intensity of emotions surrounding her death I refuse to suffer again.

"She made her choice. The waiting for the end has begun for you, Rob," Death said, and his voice was bleaker than ever before. "Are you ready for it?"

"I miss her, Death," I said. "And I miss the youthful energy of a billion years ago."

"I told you then, all must end someday."

"And after that, what happens then?"

"Who can say? An end to it all?"

"Surely that can't be all?"

"Stay, find out. Or accept it for what it is."

A cup adorned with endless spirals and curls appears in space before my face. "Symbols, Death? What—are you ill or something?"

"I would like to make clear this is my final offer. There will be no next time. This is a way out. Give it up already."

I pushed the cup away. "You can't guarantee that I'll see Jeanie again, can you?"

Death shook its head in an oddly sad way. At least, that's how I experienced it. I once caught Death joking, so I think he, she or it knows feelings at least.

"It's goodbye then, Death. I'm staying until the last lights go out. I've waited so long, billions of years, more..." I shrugged.

"As you please, Rob. You are the only one who ever denied me for such a long time. Farewell." With those words Death disappeared. I remained in the deep emptiness between the star systems, connected to the life there, but aware of the slow ebbing of energy toward the inevitable ending. Jeanie was on my mind, often.

Max and I sat on the barren mountain where once the blind, deaf-mute beast lived. He has been fidgety lately, restless, as if bored. There's not much to see any more in the universe and the last billion years the lights went out, one by one. Some light sources that are still visible died millions of years ago, the un-light a memory of a bright, energetic youth.

"You feel it too, don't you, boy?" I scratched behind his ears and stroked his back. He no longer wagged. We were lonely, even together. Connectedness with the universe such as I once had, the golden strands I saw everywhere— it's all gone now. Most life has died and even the single celled organisms are having a tough time holding out with energy levels dropping ever lower and absolute zero approaching fast.

I felt his presence before I saw him. "I thought you wouldn't visit anymore, Death."

Death appeared from behind a black rock. "I would no longer offer oblivion. But that was all I promised."

"You look old, Death, tattered."

Death grinned. Its teeth were grey and crumbling, not the proud white of the past. The deep glow I once witnessed in its eyes had faded like the fires of the universe. "Everything ends, like I once told you."

"Including Death? The omega?"

Death sat next to me. "Nothing is impossible."

"I just talked to Max about being bored. We're lonely these days." I looked around, but Max was nowhere.

"He accepted my offer," Death said.

"Dammit, you promised, Death."

"I promised you. I'm not offering. But Max was tired, so tired."

I nodded. "I can't blame him. Sure will miss him."

"We're witnessing the last twitches of the universe. Its real death is still a billion years out."

"If it's the last I see, I want to witness it."

"I thought so. That's why I'm here. Everything is gone; everyone has disappeared, except you and me there is no one, and this universe can reach its conclusion in total darkness."

I shrugged; "Whatever you say."

Death looked at me with its empty sockets. "Will you carry my burden?"

Even at the end, having seen it all, having experienced just about everything, Death managed to surprise me. "Can I? I mean: why would you want that?"

"I've been here a few billion years longer than you. In many ways, you have come to resemble me; connected to all the life in the universe. Now that life is gone I see no more use for myself."

"Oblivion?"

"Yes, though someone needs to switch off the light, so to say, at the very end."

"If you must switch it off, then the universe desires an end to itself. Is that it?"

Death remained silent. "There is more. Much more. Explaining it will be too hard. You'll have to experience it, be it."

I did not need to think for very long. "Go on. Go. I'll hold the fort."

"Farewell, Rob, be well. Thank you."

The transformation was immediate. One moment I was a disembodied spirit, the next I held a scythe. The knowledge and experience of Death was now mine and the depth was unsettling. The memories of the earliest beginnings were glorious, filled with promise, growth and unfettered energy. For Death, life was life, and the absence of life was unimaginable. It did happen in the end and even Death doubted its existence in the universe.

The broadening of my perception, once again, taught me more. Time was a construct. The universe was a Moebius loop, yet no more than the gentle chafing of higher dimensional curtains of meta-reality.

I considered going back in time, using my newfound powers to influence events, such as warning my living self to visit a doctor. It would mean all I had seen and learned would never take place. There were rules, paradoxes to avoid.

What was my alternative? Waiting for the end? Alone? I understood Death's desire to end it here, now. Even Death did not know what the end would bring, that piece remained in shadows.

The universe had hardly chilled further when I decided my course of action.

"I once promised to be there for you, in life as in death, forever," I told Jeanie. She looked like I remembered her, young, energetic, strong. Behind us was the hospital bed with her dead body, only just deceased. I noticed the hazy figure of the Rob I once was, Max by his side.

Time crawled by at a snail's pace. On purpose, for I only had a fraction of a second. "Do you remember, Jeanie? The day we married?"

"I recognize you, Rob, I feel it's you, even if you look... rather pale." She smiled. "I remember those being mutual vows."

I laughed at her. It was good to hear her voice again. "I have little to offer except our being together at the end of the universe, far from the here and now," I said. "And enough time to tell you all about our children, grandchildren and all their descendants." I offered her my arm, still in that same fraction of a second, just before Death of then would show itself.

Jeanie smiled her broadest smile and hooked her arm in mine. "I could not ask for a better ending. Take me with you."

Roger Cowin

The Watcher in the Dark

Since they began, I have not yet discovered any preconditions that augur the onset of a visit. Weeks, even months may pass while my routine ambles along its mundane, uneventful course. Then one night I will glance toward the French patio doors and there he will be - as squat and repulsive as ever, a surreal nightmare straight out of Kafka, staring through the glass. Sometimes the visit last only minutes, other times they continue for hours dragging into the wee hours of the morning before inexplicably vanishing, leaving no evidence it ever existed.

I have yet to determine the origin of the visitor. I do not know if it is spectral or alien in nature. Perhaps it is both, but I have no doubt it is not of this world. The thing resembles most those stone gargoyles adorning the façade of medieval churches. Standing no more than a meter high, its thick, misshapen body, chiseled with thick muscles; it appears hewn from solid rock, and dressed out in leathery skin. A pair of membranous, bat-like wings protrudes from its back; vulpine ears and a heavy, cragged face complete the menacing appearance. By my own conclusion, from years of intense study, the thing is interdimensional *and* extraterrestrial, able to travel between dimensions as easily as it moves between the stars.

I trace its arrival from an event that occurred one peculiar, January night a decade ago. Though I am still uncertain whether it was reality or madness, I am positive the visitations began very soon after that inexplicable night. I was outside in the backyard, enjoying the unseasonably warm weather with Rooster – my rather mangy looking mutt of no discernible breed but possessed of an agreeable disposition that made him an ideal companion for a recluse like me. A full moon, perfect for stargazing, brightly lighted the sky.

I had just located Cassiopeia and was searching for Pegasus when the stars began to reconfigure themselves into strange, disturbing patterns. I thought, at first, it was some odd hallucination brought on by a general paroxysm of the condition that had plagued me most of my life. You see, I have always been of a nervous disposition, even as a child I was prone to night terrors and a litany of phobias that enriched the coffers of many of the local psychiatrists, a condition that had only worsened since the passing of my mother.

As I played a game of interstellar connect-the-dots with the stars, trying to make sense of this new nocturnal configuration, I realized they formed a face – the face of some terrible, eldritch being, something from beyond time or space. I felt its malignant gaze staring down on our world, hungry and angry, hating everything it saw. I rubbed my eyes, trying to scrape away this mad vision, but the thing remained there, obdurately glaring down on me. In my mind, I could imagine this fiend, hurdling like hellfire through the cold, fathomless gulfs of space, an ancient, cosmic evil coming home after aeons traveling the vast empty wastelands between planets. Millennia ago, men had worshipped this thing, sacrificing the innocent to feed its ravenous hunger. Maybe it fled in the wake of stronger gods, maybe some potent ritual banished it to the cold, outer regions of the universe or maybe it just grew bored with man's pitiful worship and went in search of tastier meat. Now its time was coming around again, anxious to bathe in the earth's dark blood.

Rooster, my canine companion, was just as affected as I was. A few cautious barks gave way to a low, pitiful whine as he clambered behind my legs, trembling and incapable of containing his bowels or bladder.

As the Hunger God's hateful, alien face eclipsed the night sky, a sense of my own insignificance crept over me. I watched for as long as I could endure, until I felt my mind was at its breaking point. Snatching Rooster up in my arms, I raced back into the house, drew all the blinds and waited for Hell to arrive.

Even in the well-lit confines of my own home, I felt no safer. I could still feel the thing out there—watching, waiting, searching. Any chance of sleep was long gone and for hours, I sat trembling, dawn an eternity away. It was not until I saw pale, winter light breaking through the curtains, did the fear lessen. Never was there so blessed a morning.

Not quite ready to face the outside, I brewed strong coffee and flipped through the television news. Once reassured the world was still rotating on its wobbly axis and there were no reports of mysterious objects in the sky, I leashed up Rooster and took him outside for our morning constitutional. The air was clean and crisp, just enough bite to clear the last of the malingering cobwebs from my head. There was no sign of the awful vision from the previous night. A golden red sun broke the canopy of blue-tinged clouds and even Rooster appeared in good spirits, prancing about and yipping at the squirrels. Only when I attempted to re-enter the house via the rear entrance did Rooster display any trepidation; hunkering down with all four paws planted firmly on the frozen ground. Rooster's reluctance forced me to walk him around the house to the front door, much to Rooster's good-natured relief, who wagged his tail and tramped along beside me, happy to extend his walk.

Except for Rooster's aversion to the back steps, which I put down to normal, canine idiosyncrasies, nothing else odd or untoward occurred for the rest of the week. Eventually, I dismissed the incident as a hallucination or a bad dream.

My house was a modest, single story ranch situated on several acres. I lived in this unassuming, suburban home most of my life, first with my mother and later, after her passing, either alone or with a pet or two. Despite Rooster's sudden dislike for the rear deck, it was no real hardship traipsing around the side to the front as long as the good weather continued to hold. Should a sizable snowfall occur, Rooster would just have to get over his new phobia.

It was not until at least a week passed, though surely not more than ten days, before the watcher first appeared outside the patio doors.

As I believe, I said earlier, there was not any indication of things being out of the ordinary. I went about my usual evening routine of supper followed by a few hours of light reading and scanning social media sites on my computer, which were, for all intents and purposes, my sole source of contact with the outer world. Near midnight, my leaden eyes and bobbing head signaled it was past time for bed. I shut down the computer, gave my limbs a good long stretch before wandering from room to room, turning off lights and checking the doors.

As I entered the dining room to lock the patio doors, my preparations came to an abrupt halt. Just outside the doors crouched the hideous figure of the watcher. I have already described the little brute sufficiently so I will not bore you with further details; suffice to say the marrow froze in my bones and I felt my heart stutter as it skipped a few beats. The blood rushed from my face and I was vaguely aware a thin trickle of urine ran down my leg. Every sound, every smell was amplified a hundredfold, even my sight seemed sharpened and I could make out every horrible detail of the thing despite it being cloaked in almost total darkness. Worst of all, I knew the door to be unlocked. There was nothing preventing the beast from coming in if it so chose.

Fear surged through me in crippling peristaltic waves, leaving me utterly incapable of rational thought. The same terror that urged me to turn and flee this abomination kept me frozen in place. Too afraid to run, too afraid to stay, like prey in the midst predation, I remained immobile, my eyes locked on the dreadful thing.

An old poem my mother used to read to me when I was a child occurred to me; *"and the gobble-uns 'af gits you ef you don't watch out."* Unsettling for a sensitive, precocious child afflicted with an overly active imagination and a penchant for bad dreams. I was not quite sure what a gobble-un was, but the thought of them showing up at my door, ready to snatch me away infiltrated many of my childhood nightmares. The thing outside my doors looked very much the way I imagined those poetic gobble-uns. I did not know where it would take me if it did *gits* me, but I was certain it was worse than anything I could dream.

How long did I stand there, staring at the mute, unmoving monstrosity; I could not say. How long did I remain, even after it had vanished? Again, I do not know. I only know that at some point I became aware that the creature was gone. I did not see it disappear or take its leave. One moment it was there and then, it was not. It was not until I noticed a light snow falling that I realized I was alone. Hastily, before my nerves could fail me, I rushed to the doors turned the lock and pulled the blinds.

Rooster had quite wisely hidden behind the couch, but eventually joined me on the sofa where I spent the long hours before dawn, every light in the house blazing, and listening to the wind whip around the house. While it was only wind, at times, it sounded like voices whispering, calling my name, teasing me to come out and play and, strangely enough, I fancied I heard the sound of a flute playing, wee and far. Below even the sound of the music, were voices, some laughing and crying, others singing and screaming. Perhaps, I was simply hearing voices coming from nearby homes or even radio signals due to one of those curious atmospheric anomalies that one hears about from time to time. Alternatively, perhaps it was the soundtrack to Hell, leaking out through some occult rip in the fabric of reality. I only know that I covered my ears with my hands to shut them out, then plugged them with cotton for fear they would drive me mad.

There were no further incidents that night, nor the next or the night after that one, until it seemed that it was destined to remain a solitary incident. Nevertheless, such nightmares I had over the next few weeks, feverish and mad, of horrors climbing out of some primordial sea, tainted red with blood and fire, skies black with ash, reeking of sulphur beings of staggering intelligence but devoid of any trace of humanity, alien and amoral. Most vivid were the dreams of the Hunger God sprinting across sky, coming ever closer, ready to swallow the world in its malignant maw. In the mornings, I would wake, clutching my sheets; a scream caught in my throat.

It was not until sometime in the early spring that the goblin returned. It was pretty much a repeat of the first visit; the thing sat unmoving on the deck for several hours, staring at me with those black, malevolent eyes until, finally, vanishing back into the nothingness from which it sprung. This became its routine. I would be let alone for variable periods, then one night I would pass the patio doors and there it would be – my unwelcome visitor. The length of the watcher's visits were indeterminate, but whether they lasted five minutes or five hours, once the thing vanished it would return no more to vex me *on that* particular night.

As the years crept by, I began to ignore the visits, often going to bed while it lurked outside my doors, refusing to let any witless phantom hold sway over me. Other nights I would blank out and awaken, bewildered and frightened, unsure of exactly when or where I had lost track of time but uncomfortably convinced that something unpleasant had occurred, something I felt it best I not remember. Mostly I remained aware of my visitor's presence but determinedly ignored it, going about my night as if its foul presence did not haunt my doorstep. Even Rooster came to lose interest in the thing, barely acknowledging its presence with the briefest glance or a low, token growl.

In the course of time, my faithful companion grew old and weak and it became necessary to put him down. Having grown used to canine companionship, I quickly adopted another dog from the local shelter. Though larger and of a more fearsome temperament, Socrates too grew used to the goblin and would even wag his tail in greeting when it appeared.

Sometimes, anger got the best of me and I would find myself arguing or threatening the watcher. Demanding it reveal its purpose, to explain why it tormented me. Why did it choose me, of all the earth's inhabitants, to haunt by its uncanny presence? Finally, I would fall to my knees, pleading for it to give some sign it heard me, was aware I existed, just some slight movement to acknowledge that it understood anything I was saying. Still, it would only stare at me, mute and unmoving. Never once did it utter so much as a single word or demonstrate the slightest indication of my existence. However, for the most part, the thing remained nothing more than a temporary nuisance, just another aspect of my strange, solitary life.

Thus did my life progress, one that I fully expected to continue unchanged. I remained reclusive, living comfortably, if somewhat frugally, off the inheritance my mother had left me, venturing out only to purchase what bare essentials I needed from a small, local grocer or to attend physician's appointments. I had no family nearby, no friends of which to speak, only a few social acquaintances whose names I barely knew. This might seem a lonely, fruitless existence but I found it agreeable. I had my books and music to keep me occupied, as well as the company of Rooster, and later Socrates, so I never felt my life unduly harsh. I was very much content, despite the occasional visits from my goblin. At least I felt that way until today.

The summer has curiously harsh and unpredictable, as everyone is aware. Storms and an unseasonable cold stretch have many whispering of secret, atmospheric experiments by the government. The_High Frequency Active Aurora Research Program, or HAARP, is a frequent topic in the news. There has even been talk of alien interference.

I normally take such conspiratorial debates with a grain of salt but since the start of the year, the watcher's visits have increased exponentially, sometimes as often as two or three a week. Not only have they increased in frequency, they come ever earlier in the evening hours, beginning even before the last dwindling light of day fades on the horizon.

Yesterday, it arrived well before dusk.

Angry, black clouds rolled into the area just before dawn and had been threatening to erupt all day long. By noon, the sky was as dark as midnight. The National Weather Service issued severe thunderstorm and tornado warnings for most of the Midwest and East coast. I set out a number of candles and spare flashlights in advance of power outages but needed to make one final run out to the shed for spare kerosene before the storm hit.

I glanced anxiously at the ominous sky, noting the roiling grey underbelly of the clouds so often indicative to the presence of tornados. I watched intently for several minutes to ascertain the direction of the storm. Then, before my eyes, the cloud coalesced into the very face of the being I had last seen a decade before. Such was the terror that coursed through my limbs; I steadied myself against a utility post to keep from collapsing. There was no doubt in my mind this time as to what I was seeing. The beast appeared to be laughing and I understood it was riding the cloud like a chariot across the sky. The long voyage across space had ended - it was home. After countless aeons, it was finally home. Its time was now and nothing could stop it from reclaiming its rightful dominion over the earth.

Forgetting the kerosene, I went back inside and locked the doors just as the visitor arrived, settling into its usual spot on the deck. Instead of hiding or going about my business as was my wont I sat myself, Indian style, on the floor in front of the patio doors. As the long shadows crept towards night and the storm outside raged, we sat staring into each other's eyes, counting down humankind's apocalyptic, final hours.

From the living room, I can hear the low murmur of the television. Already the panic has begun. Militaries throughout the world are mobilizing to fight this terror from beyond space and time. There are reports of wide-scale madness, suicide and murder, of strange beings appearing all over the globe. In Innsmouth, Massachusetts, the entire population shed their clothes and walked into the sea whilst the citizens of Goatswood, a small English village, had murdered all the town's children under twelve years of age in a mass ritual sacrifice to a being that referred to as *Glaaki*. The most terrifying reports came from the South Pacific where an amphibious, winged behemoth has risen from the depths and was destroying everything in its path. So far, no weapon has had any effect upon this Prometheus from the sea.

Outside my tiny house, more of the squat, ugly goblins are arriving –dozens, maybe hundreds, swarming across the house, the yard. I can hear their voices, whispering inside my head - ancient and evil, telling me that I am *the chosen*. I will be *their* witness, the lone chronicler of man's fate.

We do not have long before we are the dream they tell to frighten their children as they creep through the primordial ooze of their brave, new world.

A. Henry Keene

Bailey

Every Saturday morning for the past two months, Bailey followed Nathan Long to the spot where he had raped her. While he walked along the rutted shore of the Ohio River, she kept herself hidden in the trees on the slope above. When he performed his rites to commemorate the event and sanctify the place with his seed, she watched and cried.

Since the rape, she had suffered a year of depression and despair, but a few months ago she took up archery, and she gradually climbed from the pit of suicidal thoughts and redirected her mind from self-destruction to vengeance. She had so much to avenge. First she would kill Nathan. Then she would kill her father.

Bailey, obscured by trees, looks down the arrow toward Nathan. When she releases the shaft, she will no longer be his victim. She will have punished him most severely for reducing her to his plaything.

She watches him between trees and waits to release her rage in the form of an aluminum shaft, and its three feather fletches and its razor-sharp head. She longs to see it fly toward him like a wrathful demon freed from the confines of her withering heart. She aches to see it penetrate his chest. First, she must see his eyes when he recognizes her and the justice she intends to visit upon him. Perhaps he will look down. Perhaps his chin will quiver. Nothing would please her more.

Years ago, her mother had an affair. When her father found out, he slapped her mother's face and beat her with his belt. Though she begged, he said there would be no parting of ways. She was his, and she would walk his path to the end.

His path was always the same. Crack open the cheap beers and rekindle the rage until the beating commenced, and Bailey, hiding in her room, would hear every slap, every body blow, and every lash of the black leather strap.

Bailey watched her father beat the beauty and health and spirit from her mother, and she devised a plan to kill him. The plot sprung into her eleven-year-old mind, and, over the years, she refined the childish notion into something that might work. She would have to do it soon. Mom was jittery and ill. Mother was on the verge of breaking. Now was the time to end this madness.

She was sixteen and fully grown, but her father still loomed large and terrifying in her mind. At least she had her license and a car with a length of rope in the trunk. At least she could escape the torment of family life. At least she could drive down to the river to walk out the tension.

On a cloudless June morning the night after a storm, Bailey walked along the river. Moisture hung in the air, turning her freckled skin sticky. As the sun soaked into her bare arms, she rolled her blue jeans a few turns then moved her toes through the slow-moving water. Her hair, straight, fine and blond, clung to her neck. She lifted it with the back of her hand to let it fall in sloppy strands.

She walked farther down the shore, where she saw animal tracks on the sunbaked slope. She identified them as bird and squirrel and dog. There were a few human footprints but not many. Soon she had ventured quite far from the parking lot and reached the spot where the river bends north. This is where she saw Nathan, and her heartbeat quickened with surprise.

Sitting on the crusty bank, he wore a sleeveless t-shirt that exposed his tanned, hard arms. His feet were in the water, and a fishing pole stood by his side. She felt herself looking at him, but he spoke first. "Howdy." That's what he said. "Howdy." It was such a childish thing to say, so inappropriate and misleading. Had he been more forthcoming, he may have followed *with mind if I tear off your shirt? Mind if I grunt while my sweat drips on your face. Mind if I press you into the spongy bank and spill my rotten seed in you?*

He didn't bother.

As the string grows heavy in her hand, tension grows in her shoulder, and she watches from behind the trees him walk. Her heart pumps God-sized fury through her body, which swells with vengeful power, and a scream builds in her mind. It tears through her body and soul to gather her shame and rage and despair into one long torturous sound. She feels it deep within, as she trains her sights on his dark form twenty yards away. Twenty yards, that's the sweet spot. I'm deadly from that distance. Now look at me. I'm going to kill you. You will never again say howdy. You will never again grope soft skin with those sandpaper hands. You will never again glare with those blue eyes, which, at this moment, look up to see me. That's it. I see the corners of your mouth draw back.

She lets the string slip from her fingertips, and the arrow flies, wobbling at first, then straight and true toward his chest. It seems to fly forever, as the grief and despair drain from her body, and her mind expands to embrace the situation. She watches as though it was a stage play, not altogether real but right and proper.

She hears the arrow tear through his chest, pass through his back and cut into the water. His mouth falls open, and he raises his hands to press them against the wound. Terror comes over his eyes, and he turns to run but only makes it twenty yards before falling in a crumpled heap, resembling a pile of discarded lumber.

The festering emotions and memories of that day flow from her as tears, which splash onto the sloping shore and seep into the sandy bank of the river, flowing ceaselessly toward an ocean of misery.

For her, the world is nearly new, fresh and shiny, but there is one black cloud in the otherwise clear blue sky of her mind. One black cloud, roiling with anger; she calls it father.

Opening the back door of father's cramped and cluttered house, Bailey feels a chill travel her spine. The delicious sensation heightens all her senses, and she sniffs the air to smell the musty scent of beer. The day is young, but he is already drinking and probably drunk. Meanwhile, the sun rises over Nathan Long's corpse to slowly bake his flesh until his lips crack and eyeballs burst, and flies come to lay their eggs in the gaping wounds.

Stepping into the dark kitchen, she hears her father call out; "bring me a beer." She takes a can of Falls City from the fridge, opens it, and sets it on the countertop. She takes the roofie from the pocket of her jeans, looks at the pill, small between her fingers, and then drops it into the round opening of the beer can.

She cuts the neck of her shirt with a small knife to reveal her cleavage. Taking the chrome toaster in her hand, she studies her reflection and wonders when exactly her eyes had lost their sparkle. When exactly had her heart hardened? She tilts the toaster to see her breasts, round and full, and small smile plays across her face.

She tugs the bottom of her shirt to tighten it against her breasts, then, lifting it to reveal her hips and small waist, ties the cotton material into a knot behind her. She draws a slow breath, lets it pass between her lips, and steps into the hall.

He looks at her, and his gaze, flowing along the contours of her body, sends chills down her spine. He had never looked at her with such lust. She feels her power now. She has his attention and knows she could direct it to suit her desire.

"Well. What're ya waitin' for?"

Feeling his eyes on her, she runs a hand through her hair and down the back of her neck.

"Yer really growin' up."

"Yeah."

"But yer not too big for me to spank." He smiles a crooked smile. "Bring me that beer."

She walks to him. Leaning down to give him the beer and reveal her breasts, she places a hand on his leg. He stammers, and she smiles. "Here ya go."

He takes the can in his hand and, looking at her, drinks from it.

"I'll be right back with a surprise."

She walk smoothly from the room into the kitchen, where she draws a deep breath to calm herself, then walks quietly out the back door to the garage where she gets the two-wheeled dolly. Stopping at her car to get the rope from the trunk, she wheels the dolly into the kitchen.

She approaches the door to the living room, and peeks around the corner to see him, drooling and struggling to hold up his head.

"What a wretched mess." She shakes her head. "Why'd you have to do this to yourself? To mom and me? Why'd you have to make us hate you?" She sobs. "Do you remember flying planes with me? I can still see it, the balsa wood glider between your finger and thumb, and you, smiling and happy. You loved me. You loved mom, but the alcohol and your anger ruined that love. You've reduced her to a shivering mess, and I can't accept that."

He tries to lift his head. His lips move but produce only murmuring.

"Here's how it will go. I'm going to tie you to this dolly and roll you outside." She presses her lips together. "Then I'm going to use you for target practice." She nods. "See? I've thought about this a lot. While you were beating her I was plotting to kill you." She smiles a quick smile. "Just gut shots. That way you won't bleed out. Just suffer prolonged pain." She rubs her fingers against her palms. "Let's go."

She wheels the dolly to him, lays it down, and pulls him onto the floor. Laying him on the rails of the dolly with his feet at the bottom, she wraps the rope several times around to tie him to it. She struggles to lift it to vertical and walks around to look into his pale blue eyes.

Bailey looks down the arrow, and a tear glistens on her cheek. Twenty yards away, her father stands, bound to the dolly. Twenty yards—that's the sweet spot.

A. Henry Keene

Little Girl Lost

Little girl lost in an untended spot,
tangled weeds taller than she.
All 'round bound by blackberry brambles,
she feels a dreadful shamble
and looks for trail blazing bunny
but finds it gone.
With no trail on the ground,
she picks a spot to lie down.
Down, down down on a small mound,
she lay where white daisies do grow,
and bones, barely buried, were arrayed below.
Sleep dulls her senses and she dreams of a princess
who beckons her to dig and discover,
beneath earth's shallow cover,
a skeletal hand.
When that boney hand, with one boney finger,
points the way to the neighbor,
the girl no longer lingers
but straight away delivers,
with cold chills and shivers,
the hand of the princess
with one dirt-covered diamond
that proves she once married
the girl's father who buried
his shame in a bottle
and his wife in the ground.

A. Henry Keene

Painted Tusk of Mastodon

Down the line of family and time,
passed from father to son,
from deep in the past,
It reached me at last.
Painted tusk of mastodon.

Oh how it glistened as I listened
to father tell his first born,
from first man to last,
how it had passed.
Painted tusk of mastodon.

In violence born, it had been torn
from the slain beast at dawn,
when to the ground it had crashed
down like a mast.
Painted tusk of mastodon.

I felt jealous of his genesis
that said I'm not the one.
My hopes dashed,
a bad check I cashed.
Painted tusk of mastodon.

Smooth as a whistle, I pulled the pistol
and showed them the gun.
I was quite daft.
I laughed and laughed.
Painted tusk of mastodon.

Feeling much bigger, I squeezed the trigger,
and bloody quick it was done.

Seems killing's my craft.
Bub's soul flowed on a draft.
Painted tusk of mastodon.

All of a sudden, I held the bone bludgeon.
My father I crept upon
and his skull I smashed
with blows brutal and fast.
Painted tusk of mastodon.

Father's soul sent in torment,
The deed now is done.
His blood, how it splashed
as his head I dashed.
Painted tusk of mastodon.

Oh, how I glowered with fearsome power.
It was quite fun.
The hollowed tusk I grasped
and gave a loud blast.
Painted tusk of mastodon

Flo Stanton

A Small Talent

I first came upon the house quite by accident. A baby carriage taken up by the wind swept into a street unknown to me, even though the many years as I have resided in this city. The perambulator rolled between two houses dark and gray and emerged onto a small thoroughfare—Wilton Avenue, according to a rusted street sign—lined on one side with stately Victorian homes. On the other side was Interstate 65, the Great Destroyer that extirpated a corridor of stunning multi-storied, gabled, towered and turreted twenty-room mansions so whiny commuters might arrive at their soul-sucking jobs in downtown Indianapolis five minutes earlier and warm a seat at their favorite watering hole by 5:20 instead of 5:25. My grandfather's was among them.

I followed the carriage, naturally enough, and found it stopped in front of a set of iron gates. The distraught mother was right on my heels and, without so much as a thank-you, grabbed the handle of the vehicle and with a pirouette disappeared between the houses. Now I had a moment, I looked up and found the most elegant house I had ever seen, surely the most ornate and grand on the street. Elaborate caps topped several chimneys three stories above and cast eerie shadows past me on the sidewalk into the thoroughfare. There were tall, narrow windows with marvelous stained-glass panels. Heavy drapes intimated tapestried walls within. A magnificent stone porch swept the front and side with balconies above. Spires and iron railings lent a Gothic, almost sinister, feel to the place. A narrow walkway lined with spindly trees led to the backside where tiny windows all but guaranteed sunlight could not penetrate within.

Despite my expertise on the metropolis—you may count *Gaslight Indianapolis* and *Indianapolis 1816-1966* among my credits—I could place neither the house nor the street. I should know them, yet I didn't. I felt instead a blank space in my memory, as if knowledge of them was excised without my awareness or permission. This absence perturbed me more than the presence of the place delighted me. Not one of our group of local historians has ever presented a lecture on it, published an article, or even mentioned it. I was perversely indignant this showplace was denied me, but if indeed this treasure had somehow escaped the notice of three generations of annalists I was determined should I somehow be the first to apprehend its discovery, I would receive due credit.

The place was accessible—the windows thrown wide, the open doorway beckoned. I passed through the iron gates and up the stone steps. The shadow of a grand staircase loomed beyond a marvelous parquet floor, and the scent of wax hinted at freshly polished mahogany panels and shiny brass fixtures. I eagerly stepped across the threshold, anticipating my delight at the wonders within. As I crossed in, though, my eyes did not need to adjust to the darkened interior as I expected and I felt an absurd reluctance to continue. I could discern my immediate environment well enough but nothing beyond and only sensed a dark labyrinth reaching far beyond the length I knew the building to be. I suddenly felt claustrophobic and turned to go.

Then I saw them. All along the grand staircase were portraits of immeasurable value—not solely because of the canvases and frames, some dating past the last century, but for the visual record of the personages themselves. I recognized the Brits, Scots, and Germans who came to our fair city over a hundred years ago and carved out of a mosquito-infested swamp a thriving metropolis of businesses, cultural venues, athenaeums, and fancy hotels. I stood, rendered speechless had anyone been there to speak to. I was quite alone.

The portraits lining the stairs transfixed me—all the way up, it appeared. Many of these worthies unknown to have sat for portraits but were instantly identifiable to me from pencil sketches in newspapers and descriptions in biographies. There was Augustus Wallenbach, architect of the grand Larchmont Hotel (where the Post Office sits today) whose construction shortcuts rivaled those of modern times, and Llewellyn Marsden, scion of the local horse-breeding family known for his interspecies commixtion. Founder of the Fleetwood Bank Sherman Fleetwood, who profited handsomely from the Panic of '72 that drove dozens to suicide. Livestock tycoon Wilson James, who provided mealy meat to union troops. Clothing manufacturer Nils Faber, whose factory at Grand and Newsome burned to the ground, taking two hundred lives with it. All industrialists of the last century–some, nearly two centuries ago.

Each step I took revealed another icon and as I looked up I could see many more. Curiously, the light followed me and each portrait was exceedingly easy to discern, although I could distinguish no artist's name. It was as if these people were painted only yesterday; the oil glistened on the canvas, every subject looked yet in his prime. This was an extraordinary find: the portraits in this house rivaled the combined collections of every museum and private holder in the state. I was simply overwhelmed and thus did not hear the woman approach behind me. As I was about to stammer an apology, professing enormous interest in the historical significance of the portraits, the housekeeper, as I came to call her, swept by me without as much as a glance or a word. This was most unusual and I prepared to pursue her when I realized that by some stroke of luck my trespassing had eluded her attention. I continued my search, drawn by the promise of ever more significant portraits above.

There! On the second floor landing—an exquisite portrait

of Malcolm Eads, founder of the food conglomerate that casts its web worldwide from its original site downtown. The jutting chin, the barrel chest, the huge pate with thinning hair—features the children brought to satisfy him were well paid to forget—were unmistakable. There's Werther Gandolph, vaudevillian and builder of the palatial Mandelbach Theatre that still towers over the corner of Leeds and Rhodes, indicted for the murder of a prostitute that never came to trial. Next to him a portrait of the Theatre itself—large, looming, painstakingly restored by the Indianapolis Thalia Society, of which I am a proud member. Congressman Murdoch, the great reformer who died a syphilitic lunatic. The higher I ranged, the more important personages became visible. The life's work of some is still extant, although that of most have passed.

The ladies were not to be ignored. Evangelical preacher Elise Quinn brought as many to Jesus as Whitefield or Finney, but proved too fond of God's own medicine. There was Miss Sadie Carlisle, whose bike messenger service furnished escorts for lonely businessmen. Minister of Health Edith Conger, provider of solutions to unmarried ladies with a problem.

I turned to speak to a companion I knew was not there—to tell anyone of this extraordinary find—and saw below, on the first floor, a lady in blue speaking to the housekeeper. She was of slender frame, with blonde or graying hair pulled to the top of her head; a person of grace and manners. She gestured with an air of authority and held her head, as does a woman of nobility, so naturally I assumed she was the mistress of the house. I leaned over the railing to speak to her, if only to introduce myself, and offer an explanation of my intrusive presence as I made my way down the stairs. I put this plan into effect but upon the first turn of the stairs, I leaned over again, and both figures were gone. Had I offended them? Had they disappeared to call the authorities? Somehow, I thought not but instead felt welcomed in their home. I listened, expecting running footsteps, shouts and cries, police whistles, but there were none.

I confess, I continued. Up and up. More founding fathers, each more notable than the last. Herbert Nicholson, inventor of the Palamar automobile so popular in the early part of the last century and the prize of collectors today, suspected of poisoning his partner. Felix Wittermeyer, founding member of the elite Paradise Club, where the satiation of the most perverse desires by the most discriminating gentleman were possible. The Most Reverend James Caulfield Lathrop, who orchestrated the lynching of Joseph Sewell. We had now spanned a century and I did not mark until later there were no portraits from the last hundred years. Noble Waters, Dr. Craig, D. C. Stephenson—would I not see them? That was just as well, for my interest wanes after the Edwardian era, and my assistant Gracie Ann carries out my research and composes the narratives for my books; or would, had she not disappeared a fortnight ago. The ungrateful child started demanding co-credit for my next book.

On the third floor, I came upon a ballroom filled with people in fancy dress. I heard no music, only the murmurings of hushed conversations occasionally punctuated with a snort or a cry. Here, at last, I was to meet the venerable captains of commerce and industry depicted in the magnificent art below. I made my way through the assemblage, the air thick with cigar smoke and overlaid with a nasty pungency. It was then people began to notice me. I could no longer glide among them without at least a stirring of interest from those seated nearby. As this phenomenon began when I reached the center of the room, in the midst of a number of people, I comprehended immediately this development threatened to make my exit quite awkward, if not impossible. Further, those who were not standing rose from their chairs and joined the others. Directed by the lady in blue from downstairs, everyone advanced towards me, not in the manner of greeting a friend or even an acquaintance, but confronting exactly what I was, an uninvited guest in their midst. I still had not gathered many clues to what had brought this congregation of luminaries together, other than their considerable contributions to the evolution of our fair city, but I was evidently not to be afforded any longer the privileges of an invisible trespasser, no matter how innocent my curiosity.

I prepared to make my leave; I smiled at our hostess and Sadie Carlisle, nodded to Nils Faber the clothing manufacturer, and endeavored to maintain a charming grin as I started for the double doors to the landing. My plan was to sprint down the stairs, forbearing to halt and admire once more the fascinating portraiture. However, the crowd of celebrants encompassed me and moved with me to the door. When I took a step, those behind me also advanced while those in front of me scarcely moved, affording only me a cold stare. I was surrounded. My nostrils filled with the stench of a dozen over perfumed women confined in too tight a space and the stale wool of men's suits worn too long in a smoke-filled room. I heard only the impatient rustling of long skirts on the polished floor, the candles hissing in the chandeliers, and a low drone from the gentlemen in back.

Quite against my will, I began to experience the asthmatic symptoms I suffered as a child but outgrew years ago, and, of course, the fear of imminent suffocation made my attempts at breathing more labored and my condition more severe. Out of pity, or curiosity, or malicious indulgence, the group allowed me to stoop to one knee, where I remained for some minutes, inhaling deep droughts of the noxious air. I had the absurd feeling if I dropped to the floor, as I so very much wanted to do, they would descend upon me like a pack of dogs.

As I rose from my contorted position I saw in the mirror above the sideboard an unkempt man with his shirt collar unbecomingly opened, his tie disappeared, his hair sticking up every which way, his pallor a pale blue, and the smile he'd tried so foolishly to sustain instead forming a horrible rictus. The effect was one of imminent madness. I started to cry out but the crowd had closed in on me again and the press of bodies against me muffled any sound I might have made.

I sensed the crowd on my right was not as united as the group on my left, and the thought came to me if I feinted left and sprang right, I might escape the terrible circle. It was then I glimpsed sunlight through the drapes at the balcony. Abandoning any pretense to civility, I shoved bodies aside and flung myself through the parted curtains. If I could reach the balcony, and a tree outside—

I flailed my arms frantically and a thought came to me, unbidden, that I had pushed away with complete success until now. A phenomenon in psychic lore exists called "phone calls from the dead," and I felt rather like those people who receive a telephone call from a loved one and only after hanging up realize the person they'd been speaking was dead. That thought was this: the Urban Renewal Project of 1962 had razed the houses along this corridor to make way for the I-65 on-ramp at 10th Street. With enormous reluctance I faced that I was desperately trying to reach purchase of a building that was no longer there and would in a very few moments find myself in the middle of an eight-lane interstate.

A thousand thoughts and images crossed my mind— the pleading eyes of Gracie Ann as I brought the poker down on her head, my new book never to see publication, the city that would miss its edifying contents, my name forgotten— or worse, never known—before the front grill of a semi-trailer truck loaded with refrigerators, or television sets, or some such mundane atrocities met me midair, and...

I first came upon the house quite by accident. A baby carriage taken up by the wind swept into a street unknown to me, as many years as I have resided in this city. The perambulator rolled between two houses dark and gray

Justin Hunter

Wrong Blood Type

The hemp hood scratches my face, plucking my eyebrows and eyelashes out each time I jerk my head. I can't see shit, but the hood isn't the fucking worst of it. I'm buck-ass nude and sitting on a cold-ass metal chair. I don't know how long I've been sitting here with my fucking wrists and ankles duct taped to this metal perch, but it's been long enough I couldn't hold my shit or piss in anymore and have long since messed myself. At first, it was pleasant and warm, but then I just felt dirty, embarrassed, and my skin was fucking chafing like a motherfucker. Not much has happened. Once and a while, I feel a hand slap down on my shoulder, followed by some cunt who whispers.

"This one needs to have a turn. He's been here too fucking long."

"Wrong blood type. He must wait." And that's fucking it. You'd think that I'd be all scared about what's going to happen to me, or what 'wrong blood type' meant, or something like that, but when you've been sitting in such an uncomfortable spot for as long as I have, your mind begins to wander. I've been thinking about the voice of the chick who says I'm the wrong blood type. Her voice is the type of voice you'd acquaint to a petit blonde chick with huge tits. Any guy hears a voice like that and he wants to make that mouse squeak from getting a good cock jackhammering. I almost came just thinking about it. Fucking hell.

I was jumped outside of this fucking dive bar, The Rusty Nail, less than a mile from the shitty third floor section-eight apartment housing where I live. The Rusty Nail is a shit bar, but you can't get better than drafts of The New Albanian Brewery's Ancient Rage IPA for seventy-five cents a pint. To sell it at that price must mean stolen barrels, but I don't give a shit. The beer is always warm as piss and the glasses aren't cleaned more than a quick spit shine from the bartender, but like I just fucking said, seventy-five cents a beer. Beggars can't be choosers. I'm not going uptown and paying ten bucks for a martini. I drink to get shitfaced. For that same ten bucks, I could get around eleven Old Milwaukee Lights, or some number like that. I'm shit at math. It doesn't matter; it's a shit-ton of beer.

I drank too fucking much. What else is new? I was leaving the bar to go around the side of the building and take a piss in my usual spot when these four or five guys fucking jumped me. They didn't beat me up; they just put this fucking bag over my head and dragged me to some van where, unceremoniously, they dropped me. I tried fighting back but there were just too many of them. What the fuck else was I going to do? I couldn't do shit and you wouldn't have been able to either.

I vowed to go after those fuckers when I heard the trunk open, but before I could do anything I heard one of them talk to me through the trunk lid.

"We're going to open up and get you out of there. Then we're going to cut your clothes off."

"Not fucking likely," I screamed back at those fuckers. I could hear some of them laughing. Fuckers.

"If you struggle then we're going to have to start stabbing you until you calm down. Act like a nice boy and you'll have a chance to get out of this alive. Be an asshole and we will slice your dick off."

I must admit they gave a compelling argument. I did try to kick out when the trunk opened up. It was a blind move. Like I said, I couldn't see fucking anything. I don't even know if I really wanted to try to kick them. I was all panicky. Before you start judging me, you should think about my situation. I thought these guys were going to fucking gang-bang me to death or some shit. Of course, I missed my kick and the first thing I felt was a sharp pain in my leg. I screamed and thrashed around like a retarded monkey. When I calmed a bit the prick spoke to me again.

"We stabbed you in case you didn't realize that. Last chance to come quietly or we'll end you like fucking Julius Cesar."

I went quietly.

The fuckers got me out of the trunk and stood me up. They had to brace me because I'd been riding in that fucking trunk and my muscles were all stiff. That and they just stabbed me in the leg. Fuckers.

My clothes were quickly sliced off, my shoes taken off, and I was led into a cold room and plunked down onto the metal chair where I am now. The chick with the mousey fuck-me voice came in right before the guys left and told me that she was going to take a little blood sample. I felt a slight prick on one of my fingers and then all was quiet. Well, I was quiet. There was a whole lot of fucking screaming going on. I could hear a lot of shit going on in other rooms, the low voices of people talking excitedly, applauding, and even cursing. The screaming overtook all that garbled nonsense.

I knew it was people screaming, but I've never heard people sound like that. Their screams were shrill, and sphincter tightening loud. They sounded like animals about to be slaughtered. I know all about that shit. I used to work in a fucking abattoir, Maple Creek Packing in Tippecanoe. I tong-zapped and then slashed the throats of thousands of huge pigs in my day. Pigs scream when they're afraid. Nobody will tell you that. It puts you off your fucking steak, but it's true. The people sounded like that— like fucking pigs at the slaughter. It got so that I kind of liked the sound after a while. Sometimes I would take my smoke break right there on the slaughterhouse floor and put my cigarette out in a sow's eye just to hear her scream. I quit that job because I was turning into one sadistic fucker. I'm really a gentle person; ask my mom, she'll tell you.

I heard the heavy tread of footsteps and felt the hard hand slap me on the shoulder.

"We're going to have to bleed you." The man's voice felt like it shredded my eardrum with every viciously uttered syllable. "Rh-null. You've got the golden blood. Good for everyone else, but that does fuck-all for you. I told the doctor we should just bleed you out for the others, but she wants to keep you alive. She says she's going to make a mint off you."

"Go fuck your mother, you pus-fed douche muncher," I said, and I fucking meant it.

I felt a needle slip into my arm. I writhed in the chair, spitting out a long stream of obscenities, but it wasn't long before I didn't have the strength to do shit. My fucking head was swimming. My strength ebbed with each stolen drop. Just before I lost my shit completely, a cold bucket of water splashed in my face. A calloused palm grabbed my throat and pinched my mouth open. A metal receptacle pressed to my lips and cold chicken noodle soup ripped down my throat. I choked, but the fucker didn't stop until the soup was down my throat or on the floor.

"We'll be doing this for a few days, so get comfortable," the man said. "Don't worry. It will be your turn soon. We just need to make sure we have enough."

This scenario repeated a few times. It might have been days, I don't fucking know. All I know was that I felt close to fucking death. I had no energy. The way they just kept fucking bleeding me dry was a fucking nightmare.

They've begun treating me a little better. Somebody put a fucking hose on me and washed away my filth, which was ample. They take me out of the chair and lay me on the floor, my limbs still taped together, but they're moving me around a little. The first time they took me out of the chair,

I screamed my head off from the pain. I felt my skin separating and the wet warm trickle of pus from exploding sores drip down my thighs.

"Keep rotating his body every few hours," the fuck-me voiced chick says. "We need him somewhat healthy for when his turn comes up."

"This is a pain in the ass," the male voice says. "We have enough blood already. Let's get this fucker in the game."

The woman relents. "Fine, stop drawing blood but keep feeding him. Two days and he should be ready."

I'm lying on my back when the men come and got me, lifting me up from the shoulders and legs. The hood is ripped off my head and blinding lights stab my corneas. When I can open them enough to see, it isn't all that light. I'm wheeled down a concrete corridor and through a set of double doors into a wide room. There are benches on either side of the room with about thirty people in expensive looking suits cheering and sizing me up. I see them leaning over to their neighbors, talking, and passing money back and forth. Across the room is another sorry looking fucker. He's in a wheelchair like mine. His face all fucking bandaged like he just got home from a rough round of plastic surgery. If I look half as fucked up as that guy across from me did, then God help me. Between us, in the middle of the room, is a table. On the table is a single hammer.

"On three . . ." I jerk my head around at the sound of the man's voice that had been administering to me over the past weeks. He's stout, heavily muscled, short, his head shaved to the skin. He's shirtless. His hairy torso is awash with blood.

"One, two, three," the man says. When he hit three, the guy in the wheelchair across the room starts slowly pushing his wheels toward the table in the center of the room.

"What the fuck is this shit?" I ask the man. The audience begins shouting. The hairy man just laughs at me. It's all too much to take in. I turn my head toward the door but know I can't fucking make it back out that way. I don't even know if I have strength to wheel myself a fucking foot, let alone try to make any type of escape. I doubt I could walk anyway. It's been a long time since I've been on my feet and a quick look at my thigh tells me the knife wound is fucking infested. Green slime etches the outside of the wound where maggots toil at the flesh beneath.

The cut up guy has wheeled his way over to the table and grabbed the hammer. He puts the damn thing in his lap and wheels my way. I don't know what the fuck is going on when the hairy guy put his damn hand on my shoulder again. What the fuck is up with this touchy guy?

"Survive three rounds and we'll set you free," he says.

"What the fuck" I ask as the hammers hit me with the claw edge on the side of my face. I thought I knew what pain is. I was fucking wrong. I start fucking freaking out. I was just hit with a fucking hammer, after all. What would you expect? I'll bet you think you would go all Dolph Lundgren on my assailant's hammer wielding ass. Well, you're a fucking idiot. When you get hit with a hammer it fucks your shit up proper. The only thing you can think is, "Holy shit! I just got hit with a hammer." That shit sucks.

I manage to get my hands over my face and slap fight that crippled asshole to keep him from hitting me again. The crowd is going fucking apeshit over the action, but I'm not sure why. Two fucked up guys slap fighting doesn't sound too fucking interesting to me. I grab the guy's wrists and we fight to a stalemate. When I finally get my focus back, I'm looking two different ways at once. My right eyeball is hanging out of its caved in socket. The guy head-butts me in the nose, and my whole front is drenched in blood from my shattered nose. He lunges in again, but the fucker misses and smashes his face on the arm of my wheelchair.

In spite of everything, I laugh at him. It is pretty fucking funny. Then I bite the fucker on the ear.

I remember seeing Mike Tyson take a bite out of Holyfield back in the day, and I've always wanted to take a chunk out of an earlobe myself. I tried it on the pigs once at the slaughterhouse, but could never bring myself to go all the way and rip off a chunk. This time I have no problem. The fucker must have hit his head pretty hard because he can't lift himself back to a sitting position in his wheelchair. I bend down for chew after chew of his face flesh, quickly run out of ear, and go for his cheek. I'm not a cannibal or anything. I spit out every bit I tear off that fucker. I'm not crazy or anything, although I probably would have torn his whole face off if I hadn't wrenched the hammer from his grip. A couple good thumps with that twenty-ounce tool and the fucker's brains are spilling into my lap.

As soon as that wheelchair bound prick stops twitching a group of guys, and that doctor chick, lift me out of my chair and lay me on the wooden table in the center of the room. The guys hold me down while the chick goes to work on me. She puts an I.V. into my arm, giving me a drip of some clear substance and another into the other arm that put blood back into my system. I can only assume it's my blood they're feeding me.

The hairy man asks, "What about his fucking eye?"

"Lose it," she says, not looking up from her ministrations to my broken skull. The hairy guy takes a knife out of his pocket and slices my right eye away. Half the world goes blank. I fucking hate that fucking guy.

"Hurry up," the doctor says as the men finish bandaging me up. "Round two commences soon." More bandages are applied. The I.V.s are removed and I'm plunked back down into my brain splattered wheelchair.

"Who's next?" I ask, jovially. The hairy guy gives me a weird look.

"Special round," he says. "Animal."

"Can't wait," I say.

From the door behind me comes a squealing sound. I know the sound well. The giant sow's rough hairy skin lances across my naked calf as passes me, leashed muzzle to the other side of the room. It takes a towering, heavily muscled man to keep the sow in place. The beast is slavering at the mouth. Its eyes are wild from pain and fear. That isn't all though. I've seen thousands of these animals pass through the slaughterhouse and I know a hungry animal when I see one. This fucker looks famished. The hairy man wipes his hand down my bloody front, goes over to the pig, and offers his gore-filled palm to the beast. The pig immediately bites him. The hairy man screams and holds his torn palm to his chest. That shit puts a smile on my face.

"On three," he says, "One, two, *and* three." The man holding the pig releases the muzzle and dives for the seats. The sow bellows and charges at me. I hold up my hands to keep the fucker off, but I know it won't do me any good. Right before it bites my hands off, I see that its ears have deep bite marks in them. I knew that I should have chowed that fucker when I had the chance. It's a shit feeling to know you're going to die because you acted like a fucking pussy.

I must have blacked out or something. Maybe I was dead for a bit. I don't know. You know all those stories people who've flat-lined tell about seeing Heaven or Hell when they die. It's all shit. There isn't any afterlife, no 'life flashing before your eyes' nonsense either; there's fucking nothing. When I wake up all I remember is pain. I'm back in the same fucking room where I started. My fucking hands are gone and my right leg is gone up to the knee. Fancy losing an appendage and not even remembering how, that's some fucked-up shit.

Anyway, they're still bleeding me. The hairy guy doesn't turn me as much as that doctor chick tells him to. Every time I shift my body, I can fell bedsores breaking open, leaving the shitty Yoga mat thing I'm laying on all damp and shit. Smells bad too.

I couldn't tell you exactly what happened. I guess round three never came for me. They're going to keep me here until I die. My blood is too precious to waste, I guess. At least I'm not alone. They've always got some asshole taped to that fucking metal chair. The least I could do was fill you in on what you're in for. After all, you and I are going to be blood brothers. From the stab wounds, it looks like you put up a fight when they opened the trunk. That was fucking stupid. You've got three rounds to get through. How the fuck do you think you're going to do when you're already all stabbed up and shit? Isn't she fine? That doctor chick? Shit.

Dona Fox
Last Chance in Lafayette
A Love Story

Penny

We were driving from Cincinnati to Chicago to rob a bank. Bob wanted to drive down and across Kentucky and skirt Indiana entirely. "Penny," he'd said, "We gotta by bypass Indiana. That whole state is just plain weird."

Right now, though, I needed to tell Bob something. I nodded toward the bright two-story brick building down the dark alley we stood in. "The Last Chance" flashed in bold neon letters above the door.

"Let's get a beer. There's something I need to–" A burly figure smashed directly into me, throwing me to the ground. I pushed myself up and looked around. The stranger was gone. Bob lay in the gutter.

"Bob? Bob!"

He raised his head. "My God, what was that? Are you okay?"

"Yes, I think I'm alright. Are you?" I said.

"Ah, yeah, but my foot, my foot's caught in the drain."

"What?" I crawled over to Bob. Sure enough, his foot had slid in through the bars over the storm drain. "Can you turn it, and then maybe pull it out?"

"No. If I could I would have done it already." He spat.

"Can you slide your foot out of your shoe?"

"No." He glared at me.

"Okay, what do you want me to do?" I backed off.

"Call someone, dammit."

I felt my pockets. "I don't have my phone."

"You didn't bring your phone? You always have your–"

I cut him off. "Where's your phone?"

"It must have fallen down there." He indicated the drain.

"Well, go in the bar and use theirs. Hurry, I think my ankle's hurt. It's swelling, too. They'll have to cut the damn metal to get me out. I hurt like hell."

"Okay, okay." As I stumbled into the pool of light from the bar's neon sign, I noticed that my jeans and t-shirt were damp. I pulled open the door and entered the bar. In the dimly lit room, I could see my clothes glistened with dark spots. I folded my arms across my body in an attempt to hide the dirt.

The tavern looked like a thousand other taverns I've visited. At first, I thought the bar was empty, and then a lanky woman with short curly hair popped up from behind the bar. "What do you want?" She looked like she'd just pulled out curlers without attempting to style her hair. There wasn't a speck of makeup on her bony face—odd choice for a barmaid, I thought.

My stomach flipped at the sight of her, and for some reason she looked startled to see me. Maybe she wondered about my dirtiness.

"Bathroom," I cried through my fingers as I bent double.

"Back there," she pointed.

I dashed into the dark corner she'd indicated.

The lights in the bathroom were brighter. There was no mirror, but as I ran into the stall, I noticed I wasn't dirty— my blouse was a bloody mess. I rinsed the vomit from my mouth and splashed my face. I wondered at the bloody spots on my clothes. I threw water at my shirt in a rough attempt to clean the worst of the blood away. The man that ran into us must have been bleeding.

I was wet and shivering when I went back into the bar and scooted onto a stool.

"I need to use the phone."

The woman was chewing her lip. She looked around. She had no idea where it was.

I had a chance to study her as she searched for the phone. She was wearing a long blue denim skirt that zipped up the front and an ugly plaid shirt buttoned almost to her chin. She wore no jewelry, except a simple cross on a thin chain on the outside of the shirt.

"We don't have a phone," she finally said. "Do you want a drink or not?"

"Sure. I'll have a draft."

She searched the bar again, same way she'd searched for the phone. Finally she grabbed a bottle of whiskey off the back bar and put it down in front of me, "Here, take the whole bottle. I was just closing. Take it with you."

Thing was, she'd had to step over something as she reached to the back bar and she'd done the same gyration as she came back to give me the bottle. Something big was lying on the floor behind the bar.

Without thinking, I asked, "What's on the floor back there?"

"Okay, fine, you've just got to know." She walked over to the front door and three things happened at once—Bob came in the door minus one shoe; the woman said, "it's my cheating husband and his girlfriend, dead on the floor;" and she reached out and locked us in.

"You...you killed them?" My heart beat faster, something in my stomach flipped, and I almost threw up again.

She didn't look the type. Then who does?

"No. Her husband did." She carried three glasses to one of the tables in the center of the room and filled them up with whiskey, then motioned for us to join her as she raked her hand through her already unfortunate hair and flopped into one of the chairs. "Looks like you ran into him on his way out of here." She chuckled. "I'm just trying to decide what to do now."

"What do you mean, what to do?" Bob said. "Call the police!"

"No, no, it's not that simple." The woman rocked in her chair, smiling. "If only it were."

She grabbed one of my hands and one of Bob's, "I'm the preacher's wife." She smiled and squeezed our hands. "But more than that, I have the gift."

I stared into her eyes; they were pale blue and clear. Her smile was straightforward. This woman wasn't a liar. I know these things. I was sure she was the preacher's wife but she was flat out insane. I was truly terrified now.

"Is that the preacher, there, on the floor, behind the bar?" I said.

"Yes, miss, yes, it is." She sighed. She nodded.

"What gift do you have?" My voice barely shook. Maybe only I heard the quiver of fear.

"Oh, I have several. I speak in tongues, that is, I prophesy in the languages of the angels, I interpret when others speak in tongues. My husband there–he handles snakes and suffers no harm; he can drink poison and not die." Her voice rose with pride, then she smiled, but her smile was upside down.

"Yes?" I felt there was more.

"Oh, yes. We can heal-"

"Heal what?"

"I can raise the dead."

I believed her. The chill that crept under my skin confirmed she was speaking the truth.

I spoke only to cut the silence, "Really?"

"Yes...if I want to."

Bob's mouth hung open.

The woman and I laughed. Not Bob.

"I imagine there're a lot of factors to consider." My voice was too high, my throat too dry.

Then for some reason it hit me. I found the situation hilarious. I can't pinpoint exactly what I found so funny. This was just one of those times when something about the situation struck me and I couldn't stop laughing.

Not Bob.

"You understand then?" The woman nodded vigorously.

"Oh, yes. Do you just raise her, or just him, or both of them?" I snorted. "How do they feel after you bring them back? Do they feel like hell?" I hit the table with my palm and laughed some more. "Do they know they were dead?

Do they remember how it happened? My god, how did it happen?"

"Oh, yes they do feel like hell." She laughed with me. We were both hysterical. She was crazy. I was not.

"I'm Marge, by the way," the woman said. *If she likes me, will she let us leave?*

"I'm Penny, good to meet you." We smiled at each other. Not Bob.

I could feel my smile trembling. I pulled my lips between my teeth.

"As I was saying," Marge continued, "they almost always feel like hell, partly from being dead, you know tissue deterioration starts immediately, and partly because I have to get very aggressive with their bodies to pound the demons out of them." She snorted, and then she started choking.

"Here, Marge," I held the glass of whiskey out to her and she took a big gulp then she choked some more.

"Goodness, that's horrible!"

"It gets better the more you drink. Take a few more sips." I handed her the glass again. *If only I had some sleeping pills in my purse. If only I had my purse.*

"Anyway, yes, I have to get quite brutal to bring someone back to life. I might actually take some pleasure in the process with these two. And no, they won't know they were dead. And they won't remember how it happened so, no lesson learned there. They'd probably go right back to meeting while I'm at women's study group on Wednesday night, teaching Sunday school, and on and on, every time I'm busy holding a potluck or a baby shower."

"She'll wonder why she has a round scar in her forehead– she'll probably grow bangs. He'll wonder why he's got a circle in his chest. Got to give her husband credit, that Fred's a crack shot. And that's another consideration– would Fred want me to raise her?"

"Wow, yeah. That's a consideration." I pushed Marge's drink toward her and she took another slug, almost like a regular drinker now. My bladder was about to burst. "I've got to go to the bathroom, Marge."

"Sure. Just hurry back." She looked at Bob then back at me. "Remember the two of us are waiting out here." I understood the threat.

"Sure, Marge, gotcha," I said. I barely made it to the toilet.

The waistband of my pants was soaked with blood. What the heck?! I pulled my shirt up and examined my bloody torso—I was riddled with bullet holes.

I froze.

I had to do whatever it took to get us out of here.

I took a deep breath and strolled back into the bar.

"So what are you gonna do, Marge? I'm leaning toward you waking up the preacher, if you want him back, but not the girl."

Marge nodded at me. "You think? Really?"

"He's your husband but she's not really your choice to make, you know?" I said.

"Hmmm," Marge reached out and poured herself more whiskey.

Bob was watching me like I'd gone crazy.

"You make a good point, but what about the others?" Marge ran her finger around the top of her glass—the high-pitched whine filled the bar. My nerve endings shredded.

"What others?" Now Bob was alert.

"Well, there were other patrons in the bar when Fred and I got here."

"And..." Bob was suspicious.

"And I don't know if I should raise all of them or not. It would take quite a bit out of me." Marge pouted.

"Let's see them," I suggested.

"We don't need to see them." Bob elbowed me. "We should probably go now."

Marge ignored him. She pushed out of her chair. She was unsteady, probably owing to her lack of familiarity with whiskey, but she held onto chairs and tables as she made her way through the room until she reached a large door on the back wall.

"Let me help you, Marge," I offered. "Give me a hand, Bob."

"Dammit, Penny," Bob huffed.

With Bob's help, I pushed the sliding door on the back wall. It opened onto what must have been the largest dance floor in Lafayette, with a half-dozen corpses strewn across the parquet floor.

"Marge! Are you telling me Fred did all this by himself?" My eyes grew dry from staring.

"Ah, no, Fred made sure I was handy with an assault rifle before we did this." Marge's mouth made an open square as her back jaw tightened. Her nose turned red, her eyes filled, and tears slid down her face. "I started bringing some of these people back. They were witnesses but they won't remember all the shooting after they come back. Everything will be fine. Well, except for..." and she rolled her eyes toward Bob, and I knew.

I knew I wanted to tell Bob something, but I couldn't put my finger on it. Now I knew. The blood on my clothes didn't come from Fred as he knocked us down—it came from my body...from my wounds...from Marge's assault rifle when she'd killed us earlier that night.

The back door to the alley, the door we'd probably wandered out earlier, was still open. Bob grabbed me by the wrist and we ran for it.

Marge

It'd been a rough night, and I'd have been worried about the two kids running for the door if I hadn't seen Fred standing there. He is my mainstay, my rock. Thank God for Fred. He scooped them into his arms like a couple of kittens and brought them back into the bar.

"What's going on here, Reverend Marge?"

"Oh, Fred, I'm not a Reverend." He embarrassed me so

when he gave me that designation, I could feel the blush rise up my chest to my cheeks. "I'm afraid they don't understand the ways of the Lord." Looking at the girl, I was saddened. We'd really hit it off, but the boy, he was another story.

"What should we do with them?" Fred said.

"Lock them in the cooler. Give me time to think." I smiled. The muscles in Fred's arms bulged as he wrestled with the kids. I'd never noticed his muscles before, or those beautiful tattoos.

As he turned from locking the door, I moved closer only so I could see the tattoos, and I tripped and fell onto his chest. He caught me.

"Ma'am! Have you been drinking?"

I tried to hold my breath as I looked up into his face. My goodness, his eyes! I pushed myself away and fell to the floor.

"They made me. I mean, I was trying to keep them here until you got back. I was going along with them. We just had some beer." I motioned to the bottle on the table.

Fred threw back his head and laughed, "Oh, that beer. Okay."

Fred poured two drinks. "Sit down, Marge."

Penny

The big guy threw us into the cooler.

Bob wasn't taking it well. He pounded on the door and screamed.

"Who do you think is going to hear you, Bob, the guy who threw us in here or all the dead people in the other room?" I slid to the floor and wrapped my arms around myself to keep warm.

"If only you had brought your phone." He looked down at me with a sneer.

"Maybe I did, Bob. Maybe I just didn't take it with me when Marge brought me back from the dead and I ran out of here the first time. Do you think that's possible? Maybe that's what happened to your phone, too?" My teeth were starting to chatter. I was considering stealing a beer. Ha. Would it really be stealing? Who owned this bar anyway, surely not Marge? "Nah, a frosty bottle of beer would just make me cold inside, too."

Bob paced the small cooler. I pulled my feet under me to give him enough room. He was really getting on my nerves.

"Shit! Sit down, Bob."

"No, no. You should get up, you'd be warmer."

"Oh, you're probably right." I was about to get up when the door swung open and we turned toward it. Something exploded. Bob fell on top of me. Dead. Again.

"Hi, Penny." Marge smiled as Fred pulled me into the room.

I couldn't believe the transformation. The bulk of Marge's hair must have been in a bun hidden on the back of her head before, because now it rippled down her body, circling around her curves. She'd unbuttoned the ugly plaid blouse and tied it well above her waist, baring her midriff. She'd unzipped the long denim skirt to reveal her legs. She'd also found make-up somewhere, obviously not her own. She still needed some practice in the application, her touch being just a bit heavy. Never the less, plain, lanky Marge was a knockout now.

I hazarded a quick glance into the back room.

"Oh, everybody's gone. All gone." Marge brushed her hands together. Her speech was slurred and she smiled too much for my comfort. Many of her smiles focused on Fred. "Except for you and...What's his name? Bub?" She waved a grand dame hand toward the cooler.

"Bob." I said, shaking and crying.

"Oh, yes. Bob." Elbow on the table, Marge put her chin on her fist and stared at me. "Do you *really* want him?"

I slapped my palm to my face and laughed, oh shoot, maybe I cried—I'd gone beyond fright, the whole situation was surreal. "Yes, oh, yes, I actually want him."

"He may not be quite alright, you know, this would be the second time I've brought him back but at least he won't remember all this. He won't be able to turn us in. He was such a prissy, goody two shoes, wasn't he?"

"Oh, yes, he was," I said.

"But you want him?"

"Yes, please." I laughed again. I'm not sure why I laughed, and why I wanted him--but I did. Habit, I guess.

"Okay. I guess I can do one. Then Fred and I are leaving Lafayette. This is Fred." She indicated the big guy who dragged us into the cooler. "He tried to keep you from coming back to the bar in the first place but you just had to come back, didn't you? Or was it Bob, it was probably his idea. Bob's the troublemaker. But I'll do what you want, then we're out of here." She held her hands up, palms out, as if to say 'that's all.'

Bob

There was something serious I needed to tell Penny but my messed up head wouldn't allow it. I felt like I had one helluva hangover. My chest hurt like a sledgehammer pounded it, and my head felt like it had been crushed in a vise.

I saw a bar at the end of the alley. Maybe the last thing I needed was a beer--or hell, maybe it was just what I needed. "The Last Chance" was what the sign said.

"I want a beer." Even as I said it, there was something about going into that bar and having a beer that turned my stomach. "There's something I want to–" that's when the guy plowed into my shoulder. The asshole knocked me into the road. I lay there a minute, just to make sure I was okay, then I jumped up and looked around. The guy was gone and Penny was laying on the curb laughing. Laughing? Then she held up the ring box.

"Did this fall out of your pocket, Bob?" Penny gave me the crooked little smile that crinkled her eyes and made me want to kiss the corners of her mouth.

"How about we go in and get that beer, Penny?" I slipped the ring box out of her hand and back into my pocket.

"No. Let's go home this time, Bob. And get the hell out of Indiana."

"Shit. We can't. I don't have my keys." Except for the ring box, my pockets were empty. "They must be in the bar. I'm going back in."

"No, you're not. Not without me. I'm coming with you." Penny grabbed my hand.

Fred

You might say part of me hoped they wouldn't come back.

You see, Marge and the Preacher were righteous takes, if only for their hubris. Imagine. They actually thought *they* had the power in *them* to raise the dead.

I groomed Marge and the Preacher for a long time; had a lot of fun. It was time to bring them home.

Now the kids—I'll take them, but if He catches me, I might have to give them back—they hadn't even filled their sin cards. Yeah, I'll probably have to give them back. Then there's always red tape involved and a lot of bureaucratic bullshit.

But I just can't resist smokin' their tender flesh while my fires are hot.

I do so love the screams, the sizzle, the crackle...and the aroma. I promised you a love story, didn't I? *Oh, yeah.*

Maria Mitchell

The Lake Michigan Triangle

Maria Mitchell

The Lake Michigan Triangle

It was a palace at the lake's bottom
Draped with caked blood in golden autumn.
The Indiana shore brooded with an oily spill
that was eyed by a greasy carnival shill.
Slime to slime, they talked for an hour
And the carnie divined drops of ominous power
for the sentient oil dove into the landlocked sea
and returned to the surface with a coral key.
"This opens the Pillars of Hercules and Pele's Gate
Where Tiki princes learn to froth and fornicate."
The carnie cracked a slug-yellow smile.
"I suppose I've been lonely for a doldrum while.
I've been in prison for the last ten years
for a similar affair with a young girl's tears."
The oil writhed into a wormhole of water
And delivered the carnie to the Tiki daughter.

She was a matted beast with worm-eaten eyes
Two Gorgon-stone breasts and tentacled thighs.
Her Tiki mask was carved from elephant flesh.
The carnie retched at the stench of her breath.
She looked him over in disgust so pure
even his corrupt heart was struck demure.
"You've been caught by scum from the wrong shore, sir.
Lake Michigan's Lamia will not endure
your trespass against subjects and court."

The carnie paled before the coral fort
sunken for aeons, but with sentience alive,
it grew beyond angles into spatial tides
stretching beyond the crest of the earth and sea

into the carnie's terror and fetid memory
of his crimes against his half-witted niece.
He screamed for his horrid capture to cease.
He writhed in wrath against the Gorgon breasts
Smearing poison milk upon his wolfen chest.
She ate his lips with a serpent's tongue
and burned his jaw with venom for fun.
His swine flesh fed the beast for aeons of delight
In The Lake Michigan Triangle's exponential night.

Sebastian Crow

Loving the Dead

Scratch pulled his dripping cock out of Marilyn Monroe's ass, appalled to find a good portion of her decaying rectum stuck to his thick shaft but it wasn't until the foul, gaseous odor of putrefying flesh reached his nostrils and a tiny, white maggot crawled across his knob that the full impact of what he had spent the last twenty minutes doing hit him. He stared down at his dick, still oozing jizz, then back to Marilyn's ravaged asshole and then, quite simply, spewed a copious amount of steaming vomit onto the bed, completely ruining the satin sheets and splattering Marilyn's corpse with that evening's dinner of pepperoni pizza, hot wings and New Castle ale. When he managed to control his heaving and find his voice, he began to scream for Cyrus.

Cyrus was in his office, going through the monthly expenses when he heard the petulant, hysterical whining coming from Pleasure Room 11. Rushing to the room, Cyrus was dismayed to come upon the pathetic sight of Scratch, Grammy award winning vocalist for Goth metal band The Tormented standing buck naked with his 8-inch dick still semi-hard and covered in cum, vomit and something that looked like little flakes of rice. Not until he saw the damage done to Marilyn's body, did it become appallingly clear what had happened. Marilyn had been much worse off than Cyrus had thought. She was no longer suitable to use as a doll.

"Jesus Christ, Cyrus," Scratch said, "I paid ten grand to fuck Marilyn Monroe, not dip my wick in a stinking maggot farm. *Look at my dick man*; it's covered in fucking maggots and shit."

Cyrus put on his most calming, concerned face and did his best to cool the scrawny, irate rock star the hell down.

"Mr. Harley, Mr. Harley, please, settle-down and let's work out a solution."

"CALM DOWN? CALM DOWN? JUST HOW IN THE FUCK DO YOU EXPECT ME TO CALM DOWN WITH SOME DEAD WHORE'S COOZE ALL OVER ME?"

"Mr. Harley, please. Get into the shower and get cleaned up and we'll refund you every cent. We'll even throw in a complimentary visit with a doll of your choice."

"GODDAMN RIGHT YOU'LL REFUND MY MONEY YOU FUCKING GHOUL AND FUCK YOUR COMPLIMENTARY VISIT. I'M DONE FUCKING THE DEAD. YOUR PRODUCT IS SHIT."

"Scratch, I cannot express how terrible I feel about this and I assure you this has never happened before. Marilyn has just been used too often over the years. She's been dead for over fifty years, after all. Our dolls are usually retired after twenty, thirty years, tops."

"I don't give a shit how long she's been dead. If she's going to fall apart while someone's fucking her then you shouldn't have put her up for rent." Scratch was calmer but still mightily pissed.

"You are absolute correct, Mr. Harley; it was a terrible decision but so many still love Marilyn that it is very difficult to discontinue her. At times, she has accounted for 50% of The Dollhouse's revenue. She has always been a consistent earner and remains our most requested doll." Cyrus placed a friendly hand on Scratch's back and began to lead him toward the shower.

Scratch was nodding his head, causing his long, straight hair to ripple in soft, black waves. He understood Cyrus' quandary, hell, the reason he had agreed to pay a visit to The Dollhouse in the first place was for the chance to screw Marilyn Monroe. How many people ever get that opportunity? And if what Cyrus was true, Scratch Harley was going to be the last person to ever dip his wick into the most famous, desired woman of the past one-hundred years.

"I understand business, man, don't get me wrong, but shit, Cyrus, half her asshole is still on my dick."

Cyrus nodded as sympathetically as he could though what he really wanted to do was practice a little sorcery and turn the arrogant rocker inside out. Cyrus was quite capable of killing Scratch without ever laying a hand on him, but Scratch was far too famous to murder without raising a few suspicions. Besides, protestations aside, Cyrus had a hunch the Goth boy was going to be a good customer. Necrophilia was a rare compulsion, but a vice every bit as addictive as heroin or alcohol. This might have been Harley's first sexual encounter with a corpse but Cyrus doubted it would be his last. Unless Scratch wanted to supply his own source then Cyrus and his dolls were his only option. Cyrus only stocked the most beautiful, hottest celebrity cadavers and only a necromancer could give them a semblance of life; make them moan, writhe and respond like a living person.

"Tell you what, Mr. Harley, I feel so awful about what happened not only will I issue a full refund but I will throw in *two* complimentary visits," Cyrus said, flashing his most genuine, business-like smile,

"I don't know, Mr. Cold. Sure, I'll take the refund but I was only interested in a meat puppet because it was Marilyn," Scratch said.

"Just take a look around our show room first - you might just change your mind. We have quite the selection; Dana Plato, Sharon Tate, Brittany Murphy plus so many more. And if you predilections so lean that way we have Heath Ledger, Jim Morrison... "

Scratch stopped beside the shower and stared at Cyrus, awe-struck "Did you say Jim Morrison?"

Cyrus smiled as he ushered Scratch into the shower.

Cyrus wiped his hands on a towel. Splattered with gore and embalming solutions, he looked down at the dismembered remains of what had once been the most famous actress in the world, the fantasy of teenaged boys and grown men all across the planet, now rendered into so much offal and ready for auctioning to the highest bidder. He hated to disrespect his best earner in such a fashion but money was money and Cyrus knew Marilyn fanatics would pay a fortune to own one of her limbs, even a strip of her skin. Her bones would bring a few hundred thousand and those once perfect, lovely breasts would bring even more. While handling them was no longer possible due to the high degree of decay, they could still be admired in their jar of preserving solution. He imagined some rich old pervert would probably get a lot of masturbatory miles out of just looking at them, fantasizing how they looked on her when she was alive, the way the nipples would harden into ripe, red cherries just right for sucking and flicking with the tongue.

Cyrus had started The Dollhouse almost a hundred years ago during Hollywood's golden age when the worship of movie stars had first become the national religion. By then Cyrus had already mastered the art of necromancy - the ability to reanimate the dead for short periods. Of course, it was mostly smoke and mirrors. The bodies were nothing but empty shells, conduits through which Cyrus could channel his own psyche and animate, albeit in a jerky, awkward fashion. Over the century, he had gotten better and his dolls, as he called them, could react almost like the living.

As his necromancy skills had improved, so had the methods of body preservation, but Magic could only do so much. Cyrus relied on science almost as much as sorcery to keep his cadavers functional. One of his early dolls had been the beautiful, platinum bombshell Jean Harlow. Jean had been as famous in her time as Marilyn in hers until she died of renal failure at the tender age of 26. Cyrus had paid, a then princely sum of $10,000, to have a pair of scurvy grave robbers remove her corpse from the Grand Mausoleum at Forest Lawn Cemetery, replacing her with the body of a murdered prostitute who resembled her enough to pass a cursory inspection.

Over the century, Cyrus learned that a certain segment of the population was willing to pay huge sums for the chance to fuck their favorite celebrities, dead or alive. He offered his services to famous actors, foreign dignitaries, millionaire businessmen and even Presidents of the United States. In fact, one of the first customers for Marilyn had been a certain red haired, baby faced President who was the only lover to have her both in life and in death. Afterward, he had held her and cried. Cyrus almost felt sorry for the fellow, if that was an emotion of which he was capable.

The Dollhouse had made Cyrus Cold an incredibly wealthy man. With a net wealth in the billions, Cyrus had been able to pursue his studies of the black arts unimpeded. His sorcery skills were possibly the greatest the world had ever seen and he had been able to slow his own aging down to an outstanding rate. Although he was well over a hundred, he appeared to be a handsome man in his mid to late thirties, well-muscled with curly, auburn hair and penetrating green eyes that intrigued and seduced both men and women alike. Sexually, Cyrus was attracted to females and males alike but despite his profession, he preferred the living to the dead, though he never judged his clientele. Necrophilia was just another fetish as far as he was concerned.

Giving one final glance at Marilyn's remains, Cyrus tossed the towel on top of a tray full of surgical instruments and turned to the corpse he would be working on next. The insanely gorgeous body stretched nude on the stainless steel autopsy table would instantly be recognizable to any fan of modern rock music. Isobel Giovanni, 22 was easily the biggest draw currently on the music scene. As lead singer for the all-girl band Bitchkill, Isobel, more popularly known as Izzy G., had given hard rock a fresh relevance in the past 2 years since they burst on the scene with their debut album *Eat Me*. The album had been a critical and commercial success, their videos were considered as groundbreaking as their music, a fusion of punk and metal that some wits had taken to calling cunt rock. Last year they had taken every top award at The Grammies and were expected to rule again next year. Their anxiously awaited sophomore effort was due out any day and they were preparing for their first world tour as headliners. At least until Izzy had made the mistake of confusing heroin with her usual nose full of Peruvian marching powder. In the few weeks since her overdose, it seemed the whole world had gone Bitchkill crazy. VH1 had a rockumentary in the works and MTV had dedicated a full week to 24 hour Bitchkill news and videos, including live coverage of Izzy's funeral.

It had taken all of Cyrus' powers of persuasion, not to mention a small fortune, to get possession of her body. He was hoping she would go a long way toward replacing Marilyn.

He took a moment to admire her tight, athletic body, taking special notice of the generous, full breasts, which were obviously implants, and the smooth, succulent genitals. Perhaps he was just old fashioned, but he had never found shaven pubes to be attractive. Oh well, to each their own, he supposed. He didn't understand the obsession with anorexic women either, preferring the more Rubenesque beauties of the past.

The first thing Cyrus needed to do to prepare Ms. Giovanni for her posthumous career was to replace the embalming solution the mortician had used to preserve her body with his own special formula. The mixture was based on a recipe necromancers had used for centuries. Cyrus had altered it slightly to make it even more effective, the result being the body remained fresher longer, more pliable and had the added benefit of raising the core temperature until it was just below a normal 98.6. Cyrus' dolls were so lifelike one might suspect they were only sleeping.

Taking a long, wicked looking metal and glass syringe, Cyrus held it up to eye level and examined it for any cracks or potential defects that could ruin the whole job. Satisfied that his equipment was in good working order, Cyrus placed the needle against her neck, located the jugular with his left index finger and gently nudged the needle into the vein.

That was when the corpse sat straight up and began to scream.

"Jesus and Josephine in a sidecar," Cyrus yelped as he leapt backward, bumping into his equipment table. Autopsy tools scattered across the sterile, tiled floor.

"There's a caul across the moon," the corpse of Izzy G. was saying but the voice that came out was as hollow and inhuman as an insect.

Cyrus could only stand there, slack jawed, eyes bulging like a rabid Steve Buscemi on meth. Nothing like this had ever happened in all his long years of playing with the dead. In fact, he wasn't sure it was even happening now; he could have just gone insane sometime in the last five minutes and this was all just some kind of bizarre, surreal hallucination.

Izzy G. locked her eyes on Cyrus and pointed an accusing finger at him. Stiffly, she swung her legs until they were dangling over the table and slowly rose to her feet. With one hand, she ripped the syringe that was still dangling from her neck, slammed it to the floor, and staggered toward Cyrus in shuffling, hesitant steps.

"The Oracles have spoken, the stars are aligned. You have called me from the abyss and your doom is imminent." She continued approaching Cyrus like a ghoul from some cheesy zombie flick, each step pushing Cyrus further back.

For the first time in his long life, Cyrus knew real fear. Sweat beaded on his brow as he felt his bladder go -warm urine spreading across his khaki dress pants.

"I nev...I never called. I...I don't know what you're ta...talking about," Cyrus stammered as his backed up against the wall. He had run out of room to retreat but the accusing, angry corpse of Isobel kept coming.

"You played the song of summoning and I came as you required."

"*SONG? WHAT FUCKING SONG? I HAVEN'T PLAYED ANY FUCKING SONG.* ISOBEL *PLEASE!*" Cyrus' voice rose to a hysterical pitch as he inched along the wall towards the door.

"Isobel? There is no Isobel here. There is only the I, The Wrath, The Wretched One, The Prophet of Those Who Came Before called forth as a portent to the final days. You called and I came. Prepare thyself for thy doom"

"I never called you, I swear, I never..." Cyrus protested. Then suddenly he remembered *he had* been listening to a song, just moments ago while dismembering Marilyn. But that was ludicrous...surely.

"You mean *Top of the World?* The Carpenters?"

"YESSSSS, THE CARPENTERS. The song of summoning, played while performing an act of desecration" Isobel shrieked, now so close Cyrus could smell the foul, rancid odor of purification and brimstone on her breath.

Cyrus closed his eyes tight, searching his mind madly for a spell, an incantation, anything that would reverse this inadvertent possession. No way was he going out like this, not eaten by a Carpenter's hating zombie, but as the cadaver wrapped its cold, dead fingers around Cyrus' throat it seemed he would not have time to think of a solution.

"The prophecy will be fulfilled. The Fire Jester awakens. THE CLOWN APOCOLYPSE IS NIGH..."

In a fit of desperation, Cyrus sang out the lyrics to Ozzy Osbourne's *"Crazy Train."*

Izzy's reaction was instantaneous and staggering. Immediately she reeled backward, shrieking, and clawing wildly at her head. Shocked, but not so much that he quit singing, Cyrus sang louder switching to Metallica's *"Enter Sandman."* Apparently the only way to stop a hell-beast summoned by The Carpenter's was the sound of heavy metal.

Izzy had dropped to the floor, writhing like a scalded snake, twisting her body in impossible angles – non-Euclidean, Cyrus thought stupidly.

"STOP! WE BEGS THEE! STOP THE SINGING," Izzy howled, tugging at her head as if attempting to rip off her own head.

Going for the kill Cyrus broke into Carcass' *"Incarnate."*

"WE WILL DESTROY YOU! WE WILL DEFILE YOU FOR ETERNITY! YOU ARE DOOOOOMMMMED!" Izzy gave out one final, shrill cry and then collapsed in a heap.

Cyrus stood, too petrified to move for several minutes, his back pressed stiffly against the wall. Looking down with one eye open, the other still closed, he very cautiously nudged the corpse with one toe. When that provoked no response, he did it again - harder this time. Then again, until he was delivering a series of rib breaking kicks in a fury of relief and anger.

When he was certain she no longer posed any danger and was back to being 100% dead, he hooked his hands under her armpits and dragged her back to the table. His assault had damaged the body somewhat but he was certain that his skills with the dead could repair the damage. He collected his spilled instruments from the floor, chuckling in half hysterical relief. Before long, he was laughing so hard tears streamed down his face, his chest and side hurting.

Imagine all the heavy metal, death metal, Satan worshipping black metal that he had listened to over the years and it had been a song as sappy and sentimental as The Carpenter's *Top of the World* that held the true evil while "wicked" metal music saved the world.

Anyway, what sort of stupid prophecy was that anyway? How silly, how utterly ridiculous - clown apocalypse? Really, the world was going to be destroyed by *freaking clowns?*

Cyrus turned back to Izzy, still laughing as he fished his embalming syringe out of the pile of tools on his tray, checked it for damage and leaned in close, searching for her jugular.

"A clown apocalypse," he said aloud, "why that's...that's..."

Suddenly Isobel's eyes flew open again.

"That's rock n' roll," she gasped, plucking the syringe from Cyrus' hand and plunging it deep into his throat.

Sebastian Crow

Cemetery Ghosts

We play our little games,
frolicking among the headstones
    beneath the cemetery moon.
Hide and boos, kick the skull
    and pin the limb on the corpse.
Dashing first here, then there,
    we're always up for a scare.
When mortals snoop and pry,
    behind the mausoleum we hide
and as they pass,
    out we pop with a terrible cry,
laughing as they flee, chased by their skin.
You would think being dead,
we would be sad or morose,
but I tell you, and I tell you true,
every night is Halloween for a cemetery ghost.

Maria Mitchell

White Commodore

Maria Mitchell

White Commodore

The Captain's Log addressed a foe
when he vanished with no tale in tow.
His ship was seized by two lightning towers
and a murder of crows at The Witching Hour.
He's gone to a fetid grave on the lake's floor
when autumn opened Persephone's Door.

During this one season the door appears
from Lake Michigan's sea of sentient tears
And under Indiana's sand broods the log and lathe
guarded by the Captain's hex against his crew of wraiths.
More precious than gems or a cache of gold,
Log and lathe form a curse the Captain left untold.
They sailed with him three decades across the lake
and were the cornerstone in his cross of trade.

A hundred gun barrels the lathe built in a day,
if one believes what old sailor ghosts say.
No army was more pleased
On Lake Michigan's Sea
Than the Captain's Regiment Four
manning his proud ship: White Commodore
until that noxious night in November
Indiana's shore will always remember.
The trip dogged longer than the crew had wished
when White Commodore crossed an angle of mist.

Lake Michigan's Triangle leered with a glow
and what snatched the ship, only mute pages know.
All that was found of White Commodore's crew
were the Captain's log and lathe in lieu
of the regiment of men, washed up on the amber shore;

No one dares collect the debt from Persephone's Door.
The Captain's son buried the log and lathe in the sand
So his father's soul could rest in his Indiana homeland
But on new moon nights, his soul's not alone;
The unmarked grave is wrung with spectral bones
who hustle and haste among Lake Michigan's fog
Trying to crack the curse of the Captain's Log.

Sebastian Crow

The Watchful Dead

The dead are all around us,
amorphous, discarnate,
    their vigil constant,
watching us with hungry eyes,
    greedy for the flesh
    they once occupied.
They are the shadows
    caught in the corner of the eye,
the shape in the mirror that flickers past
    as we go about our ritual absolutions,
the icy chill on the back of the neck
    that shivers the spine,
the whisper you hear in the dark
    when you think you're alone.
They are there while you sleep,
    their preternatural touch
spinning visions and nightmares
    from the fragile alchemy of dreams.

A. Henry Keene

Tangled

Like candle smoke, our fingers drift and yoke
and tingle 'til they twitch, and I bathe
in your radiance like a lizard in the sun.
I wallow in your soul and bite your scalp
'til your hair twists 'round my tongue,
your thoughts run through my mind,
and our hearts, red and blue,
pump blood from me to you.
We may need a shot to stabilize
this brackish blend of blood and survive
one body which thrills and tingles,
one mind where thoughts mingle,
one spirit which soars and dives.
We're less than two and more than alive.
We're in love and loving.
We're tangled.

Guy Burtenshaw

All in the Preparation

When the Red Devil bar and brasserie closed down, located in downtown Indianapolis near the football stadium, it was expected that the building would remain empty for months. Times were hard, but as it turned out, while establishments catering to the lower end of society were falling by the wayside, those at the upper end were revelling in the opportunities to pick the bones clean from the less fortunate. Nothing changes.

Within a month of the for lease sign appearing in the window, the old Red Devil logo was wrenched from the fascia, and the name Poftă Bună fixed in place. Boarding covered the windows, and remained unremoved until the evening before opening. If you're wondering what type of restaurant it was, the name means Bon Appétit. It's Romanian, and I didn't have a clue what sort of food appears on a Romanian menu.

My name is Rex Barlow, and I was once a chef, a good chef, even though the only job I could secure following college was at the Red Devil, and that was where I worked for three years until it closed.

Despite its appearance and the reputation of its clientele, the food had been good, but when the credit crunched, the doors closed, and I suddenly found myself wandering the streets as an unemployed cook.

I had hoped to get a job at Poftă Bună, but despite scouring the local papers, there were no vacancies advertised. When the boarding came down and I looked through the window, my heart sunk. While my dream at college had been to work for, and one day manage, even own, a modern fine dining restaurant, I could not see anyone in Poftă Bună wanting me even to set foot inside the foyer.

There was a bronze framed display case by the door, where a menu usually appears, but there was no menu for me to look at. I later found out that the menu changed on every opening. I also discovered that there was no price list. The restaurant had originally been located out of town, but had relocated following a fire. They had a loyal following, and all you needed to get a place at a table was to know the right people. At that time, I didn't even know the wrong people, so I never expected to be sitting at one of those tables. As it turned out I never did sit at one of those tables, and I'm glad I didn't.

Not having anything to do with my time, I went for a drink at a tavern just along the road from the restaurant, and at a little past nine I thought I would see just what sort of people would be walking though those doors. What I found was a commotion on the sidewalk by the entrance.

Two large men in dark suits were keeping people back from a man lying on the ground. A much thinner man in a much finer suit was looking flustered by the door. I assumed he was the manager, or even the owner, and the plan was for the evening to run smoothly.

As I got near, I saw that the man was bleeding from a wound on his head. I know head wounds tend to spurt a lot more than other types of wounds, but from the small pool around his head on the sidewalk, I could tell it was bad. I was going to phone for an ambulance, but I guessed that an ambulance would already be on its way.

When I approached the man by the door, a large hand took hold of my right arm and squeezed tightly. I turned to fend off the unwanted person, but changed my mind when I saw the expression he wore. It is never good to enter into a confrontation where you will most definitely end up unconscious or even dead.

"I was only going to ask what happened," I said.

"Hit and run," the man said. "Why do you care?"

"No reason," I told him. "I was just interested because I used to be head chef here." I know head chef was a bit of an exaggeration, but there was only two other chefs, and they worked different shifts, so I guess technically all three of us were head chefs in our particular slots.

"You're a fully qualified chef?" the man by the door asked sounding surprised.

"The best," I said.

"That I very much doubt," the man said, "but that man lying down there bleeding all over the sidewalk is my head chef, and this is my opening night. How would you like to earn a thousand dollars for one night's work?"

I said, "A thousand dollars?" not quite believing what I was hearing.

"And if it turns out that you are not as good as you say, this man here who has taken a liking to your arm, will break both of your legs and a few other less pleasant acts of necessity."

Without putting any thought into the offer, I asked where the kitchen was, and within five minutes, I was standing in a kitchen. It was a strange feeling. The room was the room I had spent three years cooking in, but the old galley no longer existed, but replaced with a kitchen best described as state of the art.

I didn't know the first thing about Romanian cookery, and I'm sure I still don't, but as it turned out, the head chef had prepared all of the ingredients before becoming acquainted with the front of someone's car. The meat had been de-boned. Taken aback by the whole situation, it never occurred to me to ask what sort of meat it was. I was told there were no rules, just to be creative and create something special with the ingredients I was provided with.

As I left that evening I did not expect a request to return, but the man I had approached at the entrance informed me that, unfortunately, the head chef had not recovered from his injuries, and as the patrons had complimented the new chef, I got an invitation to stay. The pay was less for the subsequent nights, but still a lot more than I ever earned at the Red Devil.

The restaurant only opened on Sundays, Tuesdays and Thursdays. Ingredients arrived on Mondays, Wednesdays and Fridays and stored securely in a walk-in refrigerator. The refrigerator always remained locked, and the meat always de-boned before I arrived. I always had to enter the restaurant by the rear entrance, and it made clear that my position was in the kitchen. The waitresses took the food to the customers.

I asked why the refrigerator stayed locked. The answer I got was that the meat arrived from local sources, and customers had to be sure that there was no contamination with outside sources. Being a restaurant in the middle of a large city made it a little difficult to see how the meat might be local. I had never seen a cow, or any other type of animal other than cats and dogs, and the occasional rat, in Indianapolis. The only grassed areas were the parks, and all you ever saw there were wandering office workers during the day and even less desirable people after dark. Surely, they meant the meat came from local farmers around and outside the city, and, to the new owners this was "local." I was intrigued.

It was in my second month that I decided to find out where the meat came from. I got onto the roof of the building behind the restaurant and waited. It was a Friday, and I did not know what time the deliveries took place, so I sat and I waited. The first van turned up at six o'clock in the evening, delivering boxes and crates of vegetables.

A second van turned up an hour later, at seven. It was red. At first, I thought it was the wine supplier. There were no signs that the van was refrigerated, but what arrived was in large bags. I thought perhaps that my new employer was using an unlicensed supplier. I know it happens, and I suppose as long as the customers are happy and don't end up with food poisoning, who is it really hurting?

Something in one of the bags moved and the man nearest the door let go and it fell to the ground. Another man stepped forward and kicked the bag. Something inside started thrashing about; illegal meat I could stomach, illegal live meat I had trouble with, especially if they were going to slaughter it in that kitchen in ways that I assumed would not be humane.

The man by the door disappeared inside. When he came back out, he was holding an iron bar. He raised it and brought the end down hard and all movement from within the bag stopped. He dropped the iron bar and dragged the bag through the door.

By Sunday, I found myself wondering whether I really should be working at Poftă Bună, even for the money they were paying me. I did not want to return to the realms of unemployment. I don't have many morals, but the ones I do have I take notice of. I know being a carnivore and not liking cruelty to animals is a bit of a contradiction, but there are ways to do things, and dragging live animals into a kitchen is wrong.

On Sunday, I did go to work as usual, and I paid very close attention to the lock on the door to the refrigerator. I sniffed the meat and, even though warned never to sample the meat, I did try some. What sort of chef would I have been if I had not sampled the food I was preparing at least once? At first, I thought it tasted a little like fine veal. It was sweet and very tender. As I chewed, I was convinced it was pork. I found myself wanting to eat more, but resisted the urge. I assumed whatever they did in the slaughtering process was what made the meat so fine. I did not want to know what they did, and I convinced myself that whatever they did, as long as they kept paying me, I would keep preparing the meat in the most imaginative ways I could think of. Like many things in life, if you tell yourself that if you weren't doing it, someone else would be, things don't seem quite so bad.

Three weeks later, I went out the back for some fresh air and discovered a small key lying by the bins. I picked it up and my mind turned to the refrigerator. They key could have been for anything, but I somehow knew that it was for the refrigerator. I assumed it dropped as the man that de-boned the meat had left for the day. He always left before I arrived as though the whole process was a closely guarded secret.

I know I should have ignored my curiosity, but I found myself wanting to see the inside of that refrigerator. I wanted to know what type of animal I was cooking. The only time that I had the kitchen completely to myself was the last half an hour on the Sunday shift. That was the time they ordered all kitchen equipment completely cleaned. Not wiped down or polished, but deep cleaned; every nook and every cranny, as if I was to imagine I had just committed murder and I needed to ensure that there was not a trace of evidence to be found anywhere. I thought perhaps I could get away with skimping, but I also thought that perhaps they went over the equipment on my days off.

In that final half an hour, the restaurant is closed. The waitresses have all left for the evening. The two doormen still stand guard at the entrance, but they never enter the kitchen. The only person that might walk in was the man I had first encountered by the entrance. As it turned out, he did own the restaurant, and I never did find out what his name was. The others just called him sir to his face. They called him plenty of other things to his back, but I never join in that sort of thing. Name calling always has a way of coming back to bite you.

So, I found myself all alone in the kitchen on that Sunday night standing in front of the door to the refrigerator with a small key in my hand. I looked about, paranoia building as I built up the nerve to try the lock.

"Just do it," I told myself.

I pushed the key into the lock and it turned without any resistance. I pulled the door open and shuddered when the cold air hit me. Hanging in front of me from a large steel hook from the ceiling was a dead pig. My first though was *I thought so.* As I looked about, my stomach felt as though squeezed by an ice-cold hand. Hanging from steel hooks around the pig were naked people. There were two men and two women, all of the obese variety; their mouths wide open as though gravity was pulling down from the hooks that supported their weight from the base of their skulls.

I walked up to one of the women and held my hand in front of her mouth. She looked dead, and I could not see how she could possible be any other way with a hook sticking up into the back of her head, but I felt as though I should know. I could not feel any breath.

I turned to leave and a hand grabbed the top if my arm. I looked up and saw one of the men staring at me. His eyes looked glazed, and I do not know whether he could see me. His thin purple lips parted, but all that escaped was a noise that might have been words in his own head, but did not sound like anything to me, or anything I wanted to know.

I pulled my arm free and got out of the refrigerator. I locked the door and went straight to the cooker that was still giving off some heat. When I turned, the man I knew of only as Sir was standing behind me.

"How do you like working here?" he asked.

For a moment, I found that I could not say anything, and he just stood staring at me, so I forced myself to talk. "I love it," I told him.

"Are you ok?" he asked. He reached out with his hand, touched my forehead, and recoiled. "Your skin is freezing cold," he told me. "You need to look after yourself. Eat more red meat my grandmother always told me. Eat red meat and you will stay healthy forever."

"I'll bare that in mind," I told him.

"You are what you eat, and I would hate to be a pig," he told me.

"Do we serve much pig here?" I asked, wishing I had not raised the subject of the meat knowing what I now knew.

"We serve what the customers want."

It seemed unsettling that he had not spoken to me since I had first walked into the kitchen. I wondered if it coincidence that he had chosen that night for a change, and, if so, it was not a very good coincidence, but not as bad as when the two doormen decided to break from protocol and enter the kitchen.

Slowly I backed away from Sir, heading in the general direction of the delivery entrance. The man on the left pulled the iron bar I had last seen striking the bag from behind his back. The man on the right pulled a meat-cleaver from behind his back. Sir just smiled as though he was looking forward to what he thought was coming next, and I was determined not to be part of the Tuesday evening special.

I grabbed a large iron frying pan from the work surface and held it up to defend myself. I reached the door and pushed it open with my foot. The man with the meat-cleaver dashed forward and I swung the pan. It hit his chin with a thud and I dropped the pan, the weight throwing me off balance. I grabbed the doorframe to keep myself upright, and a searing pain shot along my arm as the blade of the cleaver cut through my thumb before imbedding itself in the wood behind.

I stumbled backward and somehow managed to turn and run. I suppose the adrenalin kicked in quickly. If it hadn't I would probably have passed out in that doorway and found myself hanging from a hook in that refrigerator with a dead pig, two fat men and two fat ladies.

I ran until I reached home, but I did not stay there long. I poured half a bottle of vodka over the stump of my thumb and tightly wrapped a bandage around my hand. I went to the emergency room at the local hospital, and I was seen quickly, I think mostly because I started dripping blood in front of the receptionist.

I was put into a small cubicle with a curtain across the front and a nurse came to see me. A doctor soon followed her. I think I was in shock to start with, but the nurse seemed very familiar. When I looked closely at her face, I realised she was one of the waitresses from Poftă Bună. When the consultant produced a syringe, I wondered whether I would find myself sedated all the way into the back of that red van.

I pushed the doctor away and ran from that hospital. I did not go home. I wanted to go to the police, but I assumed that all evidence would be gone by the time anyone got to the restaurant. I knew that I had scrubbed the kitchen clean myself, and all anyone would find in the refrigerator would be a dead pig.

I found a hostel to stay in, and a week later, I returned to the restaurant on a Friday night. It was two o'clock in the morning when I felt sure that the building would be empty. I poured kerosene through the letterbox at the front entrance and dropped a box of lit matches through. I did not stay to witness the results, but I read about them in the newspaper.

The building was completely gutted by fire. The last news report I read on the fire concluded that the resulted from an electrical fault. I guessed Sir had friends, or if not friends, then customers in high places.

I moved to another city, and I no longer work as a chef, but I keep a keen eye open for the opening of any new restaurants. I have a feeling that a restaurant such as Poftă Bună never stays out of business for long. Like a phoenix, it will rise from the ashes in some other guise, but the format will always remain unchanged: Never the same menu twice, no prices displayed and a loyal clientele forever feeding on the misfortunes of others.

Bas van deR Veer

The firefighter

"For forty years I was a firefighter, mister, forty years. The things I've seen, terrible, dear God." The old man in the wheelchair trembled, reliving moments from the past.

The reporter wrote down his words in a small notebook. He was here to report on the treatment of the elderly by the staff. The editor expected a juicy story, controversial and loud, anything to sell more magazines.

"What's the most exceptional you've encountered?" he said, curious.

The old man looked at him with bright eyes. "You know, you're the first to ever ask me that question." He closed his eyes and thought. "I have seen people that were horribly burned, twisted steel, molten concrete running like hot wax across the floor, but I think that was not your real question. The most exceptional..." He rubbed his hand over his stubbled chin. "Perhaps it's time I told someone. Please, why don't you sit down?"

The reporter took a chair and sat across from the old man.

"A few months before I retired I was woken in the middle of the night by the sirens in the barracks of the South East fire station. The night shifts were always heaviest. Of course you could sleep, but waking up from deep sleep, it gets harder as you get older."

"I can believe that," the reporter said. "I don't know if I could be alert and effective if someone woke me in the middle of the night."

"I dropped down from the dormitory into the garage, along the sliding pole. Were you aware by the way that it's only there to really wake people up?"

"No, I wasn't."

"Jump down four or five yards and feel the adrenalin. Every night there was a fire was like that for us. But this night was different."

"In what way?"

"Little things you didn't notice at first, but later on, afterwards, they make you think. It was a Friday night, the thirteenth of the month. With a full moon."

The reporter grinned. "You weren't superstitious, were you?"

The old man smiled too, "No, not really. So, I gave no mind to the black cat that jumped away from the fire truck when it sped out of the garage, or the spider webs in the fire truck's side mirrors. Perhaps I should have."

"Can you tell me about when this all took place?" the reporter said.

The old man nodded. "Remember the big fire at the paint factories in Gary, near the lakeshore?"

The reporter took notes and pursed his lips. "That was over twenty years ago, right?"

"That is correct," the old main said. "So that's how long I've been retired." He looked down at his legs underneath the woolen blanket. "It's how long my legs haven't worked. But why? The doctors think it's psychological."

"What happened?" said the reporter. His body language expressed deep interest.

"I'm still not sure," the old man said. "I woke up outside, singed all over, but alive. And my legs didn't work anymore."

The reporter blinked. "You were going to tell me about something you had experienced?"

"Certainly. Since that time I've been dreaming. The same dream every night. At first, I couldn't remember anything, later on there were fragments. It's a dream about that night. Only recently, I've begun remembering it until the end. I'm not sure if I'm too thrilled about that."

"You are making me rather curious," the reporter said.

"Do you think there's more?" the old man said. "You know, between heaven and earth and such?"

The reporter considered. "I'm not sure. Sometimes I wonder, is this it, or is there more after this life?"

"I think there is. I do now." He gestured the reporter closer. "I've seen them."

"Who?"

"The others. Devils." The old man nodded firmly. "When we arrived at the paint factory everything was in flames. Fire was all around us. It was our job, so we started. We placed hoses, cut away dangerously burning materials overhead and started to spray water. Together with Luke, one of my colleagues, I entered one of the large halls that still seemed free from fire, but we knew it was filled with flammables."

"That sounds dangerous." The reporter took more notes.

"Nothing was burning, so we never considered the danger," the old man said. "Until the explosion... Luke was in the lead. He caught the full force of the blast. I was thrown into a corner where I lay with my legs folded beneath me in an unnatural position. My view of the hall that was now fully aflame was perfect."

"That must have been a frightening moment," the reporter said, while writing more in his notebook.

"Oddly enough I felt no fear then. More a kind of curiosity, caused by the bizarre twirling flames that emanated from the fire. A fierce fire, fed by fresh air from outside and flammable material, together they produce the most interesting patterns, almost hypnotic, you might say."

"Staring into a camp fire," the reporter remarked. "Like that?"

"I guess," the old man said. He sighed. "Then I saw them."

"That's when you saw the devils?"

The old man slowly nodded. Fire that had become flesh, some smaller than your hand, those are relatively innocent. But, the big ones... eyes of fire, a skin of flowing obsidian and an aura of deadly, intense heat. A half dozen of them and they destroyed whatever they touched and caused more explosions." He was silent while he relived his dreams.

"What happened then?" the reporter said.

"Luke. They found Luke. He was still alive. It was awful. They burned his clothes off and when he was nearly naked, covered in blisters, they fed, with him alive and aware."

The reporter blinked. "That sounds like madness."

The old man stared into the distance. "Perhaps that's why I forgot; to not lose my mind."

"Yes, I can imagine you would want to keep this kind of imagery from your head."

"You don't understand," the old man said. "I'd been through enough to be able to witness this and stay sane... Until they were finished with Luke's smoking pile of ashen pulp. Then they turned and saw me: The hunger in their fiery eyes, the blackened blood on their faces and the nauseating scent of burned flesh that exuded from them— that's the moment you experience true fear. I still don't know how I got out."

The reporter checked his watch. "A good thing you escaped in one piece." He closed his notebook and got up. "Thank you for that story, but I have another appointment."

The old man smiled benevolently. "That's alright. It felt good to finally share my tale."

The reporter wanted to turn away but in that moment, he saw a flickering light in the old man's eyes. No, it was just his imagination.

Two days later the editor in chief read his notes and the old man's story and said, "Find out more about this. Sounds interesting. We might make it a series of articles; delusions of the elderly in old people's homes. I can see the headlines now."

That same day the reporter returned to the old peoples home where he had met the old man, but his room was closed and, when he rang the bell and knocked, no one opened.

"Are you looking for someone," a housekeeper said, who had just entered the corridor with her pushcart.

The reporter smiled at her. "Yes, the old man who lives here, where can I find him?"

"Oh, you're family?" the housekeeper asked.

The reporter just nodded.

"My condolences," she said, "Must be difficult for you, especially considering the circumstances of his death."

"Oh," the reporter said. "I haven't been told anything."

The housekeeper nodded understanding. "Because of the police investigation, I think."

The reporter became very curious. "What happened?"

"If only I knew. I found him yesterday. What was left of him, anyway."

"This really isn't making any sense," the reporter said.

"Wait," the housekeeper said. She walked past him and opened the lock with her key. She entered the old man's room, the reported followed. Before the window was his wheelchair, empty, the wheels mostly burned, the chair itself twisted by what could only have been an intense heat, and the furniture around the wheelchair showed signs of intense heat.

"What the hell happened here?" the reporter said.

"No clue." The cleaning woman shrugged. "All that was left was a pile of ash. Bigwigs are saying spontaneous combustion."

Alec Cizak

Worms

They'd come to the cabin to conceive. Carrie set herself up in the study by the porch. Sliding glass doors led outside. Sunshine broke through the trees and turned Lake Monroe into a mirror. She read books, preparing a women's studies class she was teaching in the fall. Her primary physician, Dr. Kniddle, said she and her husband Ben should try making love somewhere secluded, away from noisy Indianapolis. They rented a place in Brown County. Her husband told her she wouldn't mellow if she brought her work with her. She said she'd be fine. The second day there, she screamed.

Her husband ran in from the kitchen. He'd been cutting vegetables for lunch. "What is it?"

She stood on a creaky wicker chair, pointing at the floor.

"Jesus," said her husband, "I hope it's not a rat." He wrenched his hands, danced like a child needing to go potty.

She pointed again.

He squinted, bent over, and put his hands on his knees. "That?" He nodded at the thick, black worm slithering across two tiles near her desk. "Jesus," he said, "it's nothing."

"Please get rid of it."

Three months before, they'd found rodent droppings in the garage. Her husband insisted they move to a new house. She'd bought a glue trap, set peanut butter in the middle of it, and carried the dying rat to the trash by its tail. Yes, it was gross, but not like this, not like a *worm*.

She stepped off her chair, moved backwards. "Hurry."

"Good *Christ*." He leaned down and picked it up with his fingers. He held it in her face, snickering.

She wanted to jump through the glass doors, run to the wooden rail along the porch, and dive into the lake. The worm didn't have rings around its body, as she expected. Its skin looked like a patchwork of mismatched, oval scales. And it was *throbbing*, getting bigger and smaller, as though it were a tiny lung. "It's disgusting," she said.

Her husband stepped closer. "This little thing?"

Without thinking about it, she slapped the bottom of his hand. The worm somersaulted through the air, arced toward her husband. She expected him to move, but he stayed still, wide-eyed, his jaw, dropped wide open. The worm flew into his mouth. He grabbed his throat and coughed.

"Oh my God," she said, "I'm *so* sorry!"

He kicked, waved his hands, knocked over one of two potted plants at the entryway to the room. He retched. He tried to spit. Nothing came out. Tears spilled down his face. He put his hand on the wall, clenched his eyes, and gulped. Once calm, he spoke in a scratchy voice. "Guess I'll finish making lunch."

She patted him on his shoulder. "I'm so sorry, sweetie." She looked at the floor to see if there were more. "Where did it come from?"

"The wood around the ceiling looks rotted. There's probably a way in for something that small."

"So there could be more?"

Initially, he shivered, grabbed his elbows. Then he straightened up, spoke in the deepest voice he could muster. "If you see another one, just let me know."

He must have forgotten the rat in the garage, or the countless times he'd screeched at mice running around their dorm room in graduate school. She'd taken care of the rodents. Least he could do was patronize her fear of worms.

After lunch, she suggested they make love. "Day sixteen," she said. She'd taken her basal temperature that morning. Ninety-seven degrees. "We got to get this train rolling."

He humped her like a child on the beach, jabbing a shovel into the sand. She said, "Let me on top." She'd read reverse cowgirl proved the most promising for conception. He reminded her that he didn't like any of those positions.

Then he squealed and rolled over. "Sorry."

"We'll try again tonight." She pulled her panties on.

"I want to do some cupping," he said. "Give me a hand?"

Cupping. An Eastern trend he'd picked up from an article on the Internet. He'd purchased a set of plastic cups from Amazon. God knows what they could have used *that* money for.

"Sure," she said. It would occupy him for fifteen minutes while she hid and finished herself. She grabbed the box of cups from a shelf in the closet. She placed two lines down either side of his spine. She pumped them until his skin stretched into mounds. Then she went into the bathroom, sat on the toilet, and imagined Denzel Washington stepping out of the shower and kneeling before her.

When she returned to the bedroom, she felt much better. She smiled at her husband, laying on his belly with the goofy cups sucking blood to the surface of his skin. She remembered the first time they'd met—*Javalution.* A coffee house on Kirkwood Avenue. He'd strummed slowed-down Slayer tunes on an acoustic guitar at open mic. Barely whispered the lyrics, as though they were love songs. He called it an exercise in irony. When he approached her afterwards, he used the word "ironic" so many times, she lost count, but he looked non-threatening in his knit cap and crimson, IU scarf. It was early September. Eighty degrees, even at night. The cap and scarf, she'd assumed, represented more "irony."

The alarm clock by her side of the bed chirped. She said, "Time to take the cups off." She pulled their green nipples and removed them, up one side and down the other. Most of the rings left on his skin were pink. Toward the center of his back, however, they were darker, *purple*. When she reached the middle cup, she screamed for the second time that day.

Her husband had been napping. "Turn the TV off," he said. He shook his head and finally noticed her, braced against the door to the bedroom, pointing, at his back. He craned to see. "What is it?" He sounded annoyed.

She shook her finger at him. "*Worm*."

He reached around, grazed the raised skin where the cups had been.

"Don't touch it," she said. "Come here." She started for the bathroom. There were mirrors over the sink and on the opposite wall. When he wondered in, still half-awake, she turned him so he could see the reflection of his back.

"Oh," he said.

She angled for the toilet, put the lid down, and crouched on top of it. "Disgusting."

He pinched the worm with his fingers and pulled. It squirted out, along with a thin stream off blood, like a popped zit.

"Disgusting," she said again.

"Watch out." He motioned for her to get off of the toilet.

"What are you doing?"

"Flushing it, what do you think?"

"What if it's diseased?"

"What if?" He held it close to her face. Unlike the worm from her workroom, this one had rings around its black skin. It was longer, skinnier.

She said, "Do you feel different?"

He scratched his ribs. "Why?"

She tried working while her husband prepared dinner. He joked, said he'd fix spaghetti to celebrate the day's "icky" discoveries. Then he said he'd make the usual—something with tofu and vegetables. God, what she'd give for a hamburger. When they started dating and he told her he was vegan, she'd thought, *great, a beta male*. Her father was very different. Cheated on her mother, caught herpes and chlamydia before her mother refused to sleep with him. He beat her, cracked her skull, and then moved to Canada. Who'd chase a man across the border just for a domestic dispute? Nobody, it turned out. She'd identified herself as a feminist ever since. Swore she'd never fall for a brute.

Sometimes...*sometimes*, though, her husband tested her—he tested her patience, her tolerance for boredom, and her ability to ignore his refusal to slow down and let her relax in bed. She couldn't believe Dr. Kniddle when he said the resistance to conception came from *her* body. When she told her husband the doctor's diagnosis, he smirked.

Her extensive reading in psychoanalysis came into play: Had she knocked the worm into his mouth on purpose? Did her unconscious assume it would clog his system, make *him* responsible for their inability to have children? Worse, would the worm avenge her mother, hand the burdens of disease right back to the males in their lives? She recalled her father, sitting in the garage, preparing his tackle box before going fishing. The clumps of twisting and turning butter, peanut, and mealworms he put in the bait section. He'd drink cans of Schlitz on his boat. When he got home, he always found an excuse to yell at her and beat her mother.

"Dinner's ready," said her husband.

Thank God. No more self-evaluation. She followed him to the breakfast nook, another room overlooking the lake. He'd connected his smart phone to pink speakers she'd bought him for Christmas. His catalog of pop folk was in full swing. Hipsters singing in cutesy voices over acoustic guitars. "Could we eat in silence tonight?" she said.

"I'm feeling queasy." He grabbed his belly. "Thought the tunes might mellow my nerves."

"Whatever." She grabbed a spoonful of the salad and dumped it into a wooden bowl. She picked at cut stalks of asparagus and clumps of bean sprouts. She reached for the peppershaker.

"I already seasoned it," he said.

"You never season it enough," she said.

They ate without speaking. What she could have used, right then, was a spontaneous gesture. She imagined her husband knocking the dishes to the floor, grabbing her, and laying her down on the table. The fantasy excited her, made her anxious for their love making session later. When she looked up, however, she didn't see Ben. She saw Dexter Cross, a running back for the Indianapolis Colts, gliding in and out of her at a solid, reliable tempo.

Her husband finished his food and rinsed his plate in the kitchen. "Think I might go to bed early," he said. He dropped his dirty bowl in the sink for her to clean and said, "Goodnight," as though he did not intend to help her conceive.

Sitting at the table, staring at the serving dishes and her bowl, she entertained a thought she swore she'd never consider—*divorce*. Somehow, their brief time at the cabin had revealed her husband no more sensitive than the squares on Fox News or ESPN. The faux folk music, the red scarf, all part of a ruse. While the pigs in the world came right out and said what they wanted ("*Hey baby, let's fuck*"), men like her husband dressed metrosexual and *literally* danced around the subject. Ultimately, they utilized women the same exact way: Cook, clean, screw, rinse and repeat.

She left her dishes on the table and made her way to the bedroom. Her husband was under the covers. "Oh good," he said. "Could you turn off the lights for me?"

"Sweets?" she said.

He didn't respond.

"Excuse me?"

He sighed. "I'm here."

"Did you forget? We have to do it again."

"Oh, great," he said. All the enthusiasm of someone in a dentist's chair awaiting a root canal. How did he even get it up for her? He kicked his covers off and slid out of his boxers. "My stomach's killing me."

She took her jeans and t-shirt off. Folded them and put them on a wooden chair near her side of the bed. She stepped out of her panties and placed them on top of a wicker nightstand. She left her bra on. Her husband hadn't played with her breasts in a year. She joked once that she'd have them "done." He'd shrugged and said, "If that makes *you* happy, go ahead and get the surgery."

Laying down next to him, she imagined making love to Paulo Tinajero, the best-looking member of the American soccer team. She ran her fingers along her husband's body and stopped. "Hey," she said.

His eyes weren't even open.

"Hey."

"What?"

She pointed to thin strips of his skin rising and falling all across his arms, legs, and chest. "Don't you feel that?"

"Not really."

"That doesn't look healthy."

"Fine," he said. "I'll drive to Indy and see Dr. Kniddle tomorrow."

Just like her father. He'd blow snot all over the house, bleed from his ears, vomit chunks of his insides. If her mother told him to see a doctor, he'd slap her mouth. "Stop stepping on my dick," he'd say, every time.

Her husband grabbed the back of her head and forced his tongue into her mouth. After almost choking her, he said, "Let's get you taken care of."

She wanted to scream again. The man had *never* "taken care" of her. Then she noticed his penis throbbing, the same as the worm she'd found in her study. This excited her. She sat on top of him and rocked back and forth. Normally, he'd go limp with her riding cowgirl style.

Whatever the worm had done to his body it kept him available while she rotated and shuffled until, miracle of miracles, *she* had an orgasm. She slid off him, shaking and euphoric.

He said, "Hey, I didn't get mine."

She turned her back to him and laughed. She laughed until she closed her eyes and fell asleep. She dreamed of having a daughter. Just her and her daughter, walking across a meadow in the summertime. They picked Dandelions and blew on them, scattering seeds in all directions. The world tilted. She fell into the sky.

She woke up as her head bounced off the hardwood floor. Her husband had pushed her off the bed in his sleep. She climbed to her feet, using the wicker nightstand for support. In the dark, it looked as though a four-hundred pound man had taken her husband's place. She backed toward the door to the room and flipped the light switch.

Her husband had ballooned into a mass twice his normal size. His arms, legs, and torso appeared to have *inflated*. His skin shined, as though it were plastic. She leaned over to examine his face. His eyes stared at the ceiling, his mouth hung open. She whispered his name. No response. She shouted his name.

"Oh God," she said. She tapped his shoulder. His body exploded. Wind from the blast knocked her to the floor once more. Electricity snaked through her brain. Chunks of her husband's flesh and bones scattered and stuck to the walls and ceiling. Then a black mass of squirming worms rained down. A thousand slimy fingers grabbed her all over. They smothered her, crawled into her mouth, her nose, her ears. She bit down, crushed as many as she could with her teeth. The ones she missed slithered to her throat. She grabbed her neck, as though that might stop them.

Then the worms wiggled in between her legs.

She named the daughter she never had—*Chloe*. "Chloe," she imagined saying to the girl, "have no expectations in life. That's the only way you'll be happy." The worms burrowed into the skin above her mouth. She forced herself to smile as they wrapped themselves around her lips and squeezed.

Mary Patterson Thornburg

Tricker-Treat

When people ask me what my favorite holiday is, I always tell them Halloween.

Actually, nobody ever asks me that, but if anybody *did*, that's what I'd say. What other day can you get out in the night air, in the moonlight sometimes, and stay out for hours and hours? What other day can you do normal stuff with other kids – well, somewhat normal, anyway? What other day can you really do *anything* fun? No other day, that's what—only Halloween.

Christmas was okay when I was little, I guess, but I don't remember much about it, and later on there wasn't much to remember, if you know what I mean. Seemed like everybody was mad about something, or else sad, and when I got presents one year they got busted up before the day was over. Other years I didn't get anything, which was okay. My birthday wasn't quite so bad, because usually nobody remembered it but me.

So Halloween is what I'd say is my favorite, if anybody wanted to know.

When I was little, maybe the first time I ever went out tricker-treating, my mom took me, and I was dressed up like a black cat, and people said, *Isn't that cute? Who made your costume, sweetie? My mommy did, I said.* She did, too, and she made it real good. Another time, a year or so later, I was a hobo, and that was good too. I just wore some of my regular clothes and smeared some dirt on my face, and made me a hobo sack out of an old bandanna and a stick from a bush. That time I went out with some kids from the neighborhood and brought home a bunch of treats. I don't suppose I got to eat any of that stuff, but that was okay. It was fun anyway.

The treats are fine, I guess, for those that like them, but the best part is getting them. Going out tricker-treating with a bunch of other kids, all yelling and laughing and having fun. People coming to doors and laughing, acting like they're scared, but you know they're really not. Giving us candy and stuff for our bags, and saying *now don't eat all that at once* and *watch out crossing streets, now*.

For a couple of years, though, I didn't go out at all. That was a bad time here in Granville. The last factory shut down and most of the downtown stores closed. My mom lost her job and couldn't get another one. The guy that was living with us took off one morning and never came back, which was all right with me but my mom took it hard. It was a bad time at our house too, and it got worse. Lots worse. I don't even like to remember it.

Then one year I went with some kids again—met them after it got good and dark, and they looked at me kind of strange at first, but I asked could I come with them, and I had my bag, so they said okay.

That was a real good time. Perfect weather for tricker-treat – nice and cool but not cold, the sugar maples were all red and yellow and the leaves hadn't blown off yet, and there was a little moon but not too much. We stayed out of my old neighborhood – the people there who hadn't moved out yet weren't in the mood to give candy away to a bunch of kids, we figured, and somebody might have taken a shot at us just for the heck of it, so we went up to the north side by the college and knocked on doors there.

The first house we went to, when the woman saw me she backed off a little. *Whoa*, she said, *what kind of costume is THAT?* I didn't exactly know what to say, so I didn't say anything. *What ARE you,* she said. One of the boys in the group said, *He's a corpse, can't you tell?* Some of the kids laughed. And that's what I was, all right. My skin was all kind of gray, kind of greenish around the mouth, lots of bruises everywhere, and my eyes were sort of hollow, real dark all around. I figured it was a good Halloween look.

Anyway, the woman gave me a kind of frown, but she put an extra candy bar in my bag. *Don't eat all that at once, now*, she said, and I said, *Thank you. I won't.*

As I was leaving, the woman said to me, *who fixed that costume for you, anyway?* I told her my mom did. Which was the truth, of course.

The next year I must have looked pretty awful, and a couple of the really little kids in the group said they were going home. The older ones called them babies and chicken and all that. *They* thought I looked cool, they said. Anyhow, I stayed mostly behind everybody, out of the porch lights. Even then, one man came out and looked us all over, and when he got to me, he said *damn, that is sick*, and shook his head and went back in his house. But he'd already given us his treats.

After that when I went out I was always a skeleton. Skeletons used to scare me bad when I was young, but they don't any more. And even though there were other skeletons in the groups I went out with, I always looked the best, and I could tell they all knew it, too. A couple of them even told me so. Those were really good times.

This last year was a good time, too, right up to the end anyway. And even then it could've been worse.

What happened was, I got with this bunch of kids, most of them pretty old—not as old as me of course but *bigger* than me, and most were boys. There was one girl, who was a princess, and everybody was trying to impress her, it seemed like. She was very pretty, even though her costume was cheap and didn't look like much. I was a skeleton again. Like always, I stayed with the group but kind of hung back too. I didn't know the rest of them, so that was okay.

There was this one kid, quite a bit bigger than the rest, that the others called Kevin. He was a pirate, one of those real popular costumes, and he looked really good –sword, hat, fake parrot, the works. He kept going *Arr, Matey*, and stuff like that. The problem was, this Kevin had his little brother with him, who was a lot younger than the rest of the kids. He looked to be only six or seven, maybe. Too young to be out with the others, I thought, but I didn't say anything. He seemed to be having a good time, at least at first.

Then he got tired, and he was kind of moping along, looking in his bag while he walked, and Kevin kept going, *come ON, Kylie! Hurry up, for God's sake.* Then the kid would close up the bag again and walk a little faster, but pretty soon he'd slow down again and Kevin would yell at him again. And then I happened to look at them this one time, and Kevin gave the little guy a slap upside the head. Not *real* hard, not as hard as I used to get slapped sometimes, but still. I hate that worse than anything. Hate to see it. He was just a little kid.

So I hollered at Kevin. Just, *Hey, lay off him, Long John Silver,* or something like that. But that was the wrong thing to do, I guess, because after that he kept yelling at little Kylie as much as he could, and every time he yelled he'd look at me, like, *what're you going to do about it?*

I could see I hadn't done any good, so I let it go. The kid kept stumbling along, trying to keep up, and pretty soon we got to just outside the old Beechwood cemetery there on the boulevard, right across from that tin man. The place doesn't bother me any, but some of the kids said it was getting late and they had to go home. So they took off, including the pretty girl that Kevin was trying to impress. There were only three or four others left. And that's when I saw Kevin grab his little brother's bag away from him and scoop out a whole bunch of treats and put them in his own bag.

Naturally little Kylie started yelling. What did Kevin do then? He took a big swing at Kylie and knocked him right down on the sidewalk. I ran over to where they were. Something just seemed to make me do it. Like I said, I really hate that, when somebody hurts a little kid. *Get up, Kylie,* I said to the little guy. I didn't really even think about what I *could* do about it, but I just felt like I wanted to protect him.

Kevin looks over at me, and he pulls his wooden sword out and shakes it around like he's going to make somebody walk the plank or something. *Who the hell do you think you are, Bony?* he says. I go, *C'mon, Kylie, get up.* And just as the little kid gets up, Kevin whacks him with the sword, *hard*, and down he goes again. By now, he's crying loud, and Kevin grabs his bag and stuffs it inside his own bag. *More swag for the captain*, he says. And little Kylie goes *I'll tell, I'll tell!* And Kevin laughs and says, *So? I'll say you're lying, and then you'll get it from Mom too.*

That was all it took. When I go out on Halloween, I try to stay in the shadows pretty much, and I always keep from touching the other kids, naturally. But when Kevin said that, I couldn't help myself. He and Kylie were right under a street lamp, but I went all the way up to him and grabbed him by the wrist, just as hard as I could, and held on. I didn't say anything, and he pulled the wooden sword back like he was going to hit me with it. But then he looked at my eyes. *Into* my eyes, I mean. And one of those spiders crawled out of the socket.

Right away, Kevin starts screaming. *AAAAAaaa! It's real! It's real!* He takes off running like he was shot out of a gun. I didn't let go. I didn't have *time* to let go. And my hand came off and held on to his arm all the way down to the corner.

When the other kids saw that, they all took off too, even little Kylie. They were running in all directions. I had hold of my bag with the other hand, and when they took off, I dropped it. *Kylie, come back*, I yelled. *Here, you can have mine!* But he just kept on running.

I left the bag there on the sidewalk, though. There was a lot of candy and apples and popcorn balls in it, and I thought maybe he'd come back for it, or at least somebody would. Not Kevin the pirate, I figured.

I never eat that stuff anyway.

John D. Stanton

Zero-point

I have no idea in hell what a C-bomb is; I doubt anybody really does, except for the fucker who built one and set it off in his basement fifteen years ago. An obscure blog by someone calling himself "J.F. Parnell" claimed to explain the bombing as a hemorrhage of space and time at a nexus or zero-point; it has been rewritten and recirculated so many times, it's seen as one of a hundred nut case explanations for the 11th Street Horror.

The official version is that some douche bag terrorist wannabe copped an experimental isotope and built a dirty bomb that killed about one-quarter of a mile in radius of downtown Indianapolis. Mysteriously, this freak isotope somehow fused itself to all solid matter in the D-Zone (as in, step one foot inside and you're dead), but didn't spread like normal atomic fallout. The Zone will supposedly remain uninhabitable for the half-life of the isotope, 280 years. Hence, the barricades and the fencing, the bilingual biohazard signs, and a decade of armed guards in radiation suits.

Thick black dead vines now cover the retaining walls and fencing, forming a natural and more ominous barrier than the graffiti-stained Berlin-style walls the D.O.D. built. Since the vines have taken over, an odd thing has happened—the D-Zone itself is all but forgotten. The guards no longer patrol. Neighbors walk past the Zone as if hypnotically blinded to its existence. Even animals avoid the area as if it simply isn't there. The Zone still shimmers during a thunderstorm, sizzling and crackling as if the water is shorting a vast power grid. Once in a great while a greasy black plume of smoke will erupt from its center— but no one will act as though he notices, or is curious. Except for those of us still bound to the Zone.

I was born two blocks over from Ground Zero, in an Italianate mansion built just before the end of the Civil War. The house has been in our family since 1903. During the Great Depression, it was subdivided into a number of dank apartments in which generations of nameless misfits lived out their lives in silence and despair. I was about four years old when Mrs. Garbarini passed away. The paramedics had to remove her apartment door so they could squeeze her corpulent mass through the frame and haul it down the spiral staircase. I still remember how she stank as they struggled past me and out the front door.

The day of the explosion, I spent with my grandmother, while my parents thrashed out their divorce settlement. I was on my bicycle heading home late, just outside of what would later be called the D-Zone, when the shock wave upended me and tossed me upside down into a hedge. My father, who had apparently taken St. Clair Street to Grandma's, was never seen again. My mother visited me twice—once in the hospital complex when I was thirteen, and once at the ptomaine wagon at The Factory a few years later.

I was told that radiation did something strange to my brain. I was told that the microfilament probes that spiked my cerebrum like so many kabobs were there for my own good, terminating in a micro jack behind my left ear so the doctors could upgrade the software that controlled the cascading storms in my mind. I was told many things I was ignorant enough to believe at the time.

After every incident, I was told that the days and weeks I spent strapped to a slanting table, drifting in and out of consciousness, were simply an "adjustment." I remember clawing my skin furiously with a freed hand. I remember waking to the sound of my own screaming, while men in masks and white headgear peered at me and probed me with needles.

I remember my friend Leon, a scrawny, sandy-haired kid with a twisted grin, a couple of years younger than I:

another refugee from the D-Zone. Leon showed me a secret room he found through a ventilation duct he'd opened in the janitor's closet. We would hide there and play for hours, and plan our Great Escape.

I was told Leon died one night because he refused to take his meds. So, I took mine.

Even with the drugs and the brain-kabobs, I spent what must have been years on that slanting table, wired into a machine, drifting back and forth between worlds. Over time, the monotonous clacks of this machinery became a rhythm, a metronome that marked off the time in this alternate reality. An antique DC generator nearby provided a constant, soothing hum, a reminder that I was alive, somewhere, floating in a mechanical womb.

Whatever this radiation had supposedly done to me, I was now something else: a new use had been found for me. I felt information being pumped into my brain, where it was processed in countless dreaming scenarios and tableaus; refined, sequenced, then sucked back out. Hellish things a child should not witness. I was told that war, famine and disease had wiped out three-quarters of the world's population while I was dreaming.

Once, when I'd drifted back enough to hear the DC generator, I could "see" the kabobs in my brain. Purple sparks would shoot off one wire, bound across synapses, and dive deep into the brain like lightning flickering through a storm cloud.

I imagined a metal chain, forming link by link, snaking its way from one kabob to another: neuropeptides shorting out this wire and then that, controlling the flow of data. As I pushed my fear, then my rage, into those wires, I felt as if I were suddenly, truly conscious for the first time in my life.

I saw a white-masked face recoil in horror, electrified by my purple sparks, sent flying across the room a smoldering mass of meat.

I smelled ozone and melting plastic as one rack after another of electronic gear sputtered, arced, and died, hissing.

Then there was a needle in my arm, and another, and another.

When next I awoke, I was in a different facility. I was told that some measure of a "cure" had been effected, and I was entered into a "vocational rehabilitation" program. That's where I met Leah, one of the last of the D-Zone kids. Another decommissioned brain freak smart enough to pretend she didn't remember shit.

Over the next two years, we trained for our factory jobs, matching meter and pace of the witless automatons in the program. Some were dead-eyed ex-soldiers screwed by the V.A. then in trouble with local law enforcement. A few others started life as crack babies, but most were "spike heads," victims of the latest bioengineered euphoric mind-fuck, remanded for "rehabilitation" by what called itself the government.

"Rehabilitation," for me, meant spending twelve hours a day tethered to a laser lathe.

I remember when I was a boy, reading about the Manhattan Project; how parts for the first atomic bombs were farmed out to machine shops across the US. The machinists had no clue what the parts were for, and the plans were intentionally divided among the shops so there was very little chance any individual, in his wildest imagination, could conceive of what these parts would ultimately be assembled to create.

I made the part I was ordered to, day after day. Forming a curved piece of a chrome-like alloy, apparently one-sixth of a sphere, with a grooved lip on all edges, and nine precisely spaced holes for bolts. I wore thick goggles and an air filter, and monitored the hydraulics that held the block of alloy in place while the laser shaved white-hot spiraling ribbons of metal that violently snaked off the chunk. The cheap chain mail armor I was provided with usually deflected the metal snakes, but every day a sliver or two would sizzle under my skin. I could tweeze them out after my shift, if I was bored.

Was the part I made important? Was it a vital element for turbines powering what's left of the world? or, perhaps the skullcap of a race of machine-gods? Was this brittle sphere just a new design for shrapnel, like the shredder bombs of past generations? All I would ever know was that I had to make twelve of these pieces, perfect to the nanometer, every day.

Leah worked three stations over. I would occasionally get a glimpse of her when she was released for a bathroom break. Her shift started two hours after mine, but I would see her at lunch. After "Rehabilitation," she was permitted to visit my cubicle at night.

When we met, Leah had long copper hair and bangs. Flecks of silver danced in her eyes; her voice was sultry, and her smile full of mischief. We talked, or more accurately linked about our dreams, mostly. D-Zone children dream almost constantly. Even when we are awake, these dreams superimpose or split-screen our consciousness. They called it a "hyper-sentient link," a continuous flood of images and emotions from the Zone, and amongst the survivors. The probes, the drugs, the feeble attempts at therapy were at first intended to break or modify this link. Later, the protocols were adjusted to exploit it. Those of us who learned how to short out our probes became a threat to the program, and ended up in The Factory. Providing we survived rehabilitation.

By the end of rehab, Leah's hair was chopped short. After another year in The Factory, she was gaunt, and the light had all but left her eyes.

The metal flecks that burned into our skin deposited enough toxic ions to render our subcutaneous GPS chips worthless. That was when Sniffers were introduced. Sniffers are part bloodhound—literally. These ugly fuckers are the product of some clever gene splicing. They know if you are lying, whom you've slept with, what you ate for dinner last night, and they can track you through a full-force gale. That was when I developed a craving for certain ethnic foods.

Our Sniffer was a particularly odious mongrel, hovering around Leah at the slightest whiff of sex.

The night we escaped, Leah slipped up from behind and pinioned his arms back while I shoved a turkey baster up his left nostril and filled his sinus cavities with a mixture of capsicum, Indian curry and Habanero sauce. This Sniffer wouldn't be able to find his own ass from now on, much less ours. He struggled violently for a moment while I held my hand over his face to muffle his screams; somehow, he managed to scratch Leah's arm before he went down. I tore the cuff from my shirt, dabbed Leah's blood on it, and hung it on the razor wire fence in the shadow of one of The Factory's twin smokestacks.

Earlier in the week, I had finished cutting the welds on a sewer lid on the grounds, and replaced them with putty rolled in rust in case a guard might notice. A long drop, a mile's swim through rats and raw sewage, and we were free. Cold rain-washed us clean; in an abandoned warehouse, we changed into dry clothes I'd carried in a plastic pouch.

The D-Zone by now was three miles to the north. If our luck held, no one had thought to check the sewers, and they were still looking for us in the perimeter of The Factory. If they did find the bloody cuff, it pointed in the wrong direction.

We slid in and out of alleys, vaulted fences, and held to the embrace of shadows. Hungry, torn and exhausted from our shifts and our escape, we dodged patrol cruisers, gang-bangers and junkies. We had to make it to the D-Zone, tonight.

Now the black vines loomed just ahead. We were walking in the shadows against a privacy fence, in an alley behind a food bank. A rusty door creaked as I stepped into the light that shot from it. A night watchman, an old man firing up a blunt, saw me dressed in black. He drew his gun, his hand wobbling, and he fired just as he bellowed, "Who's there?" Leah dropped at my feet, and I saw the purple lightning again. The guard managed a brief shriek before he... came apart.

As I held her, blood spurted from Leah's mouth. She nodded toward the vines, mouthed "Go," and died.

I climbed the black vines one fistful, one foothold at a time, as the rain started again. An aurora of energy crackled, and the plume of black smoke belched up from the center of the Zone. As I rolled over the top, I fell into the grid. My mind was on fire before I hit the ground.

As my vision cleared a bit, I saw feral children hovering over me. They silently pointed to the center of the Zone, to the column of black that rose into the sky. Whether it was fear or instinct, I ran in the opposite direction, to my grandmother's house.

Up the spiral staircase, past an old reprobate in tattered clothes—his eyes shimmered silver as I stepped over him. Purple sparks leapt from all my brain-kabobs, and I heard thunder. At the top of the stairs stood my grandmother— she smiled, and her silver eyes shone while she phased— now solid, now wispy, and now solid again. She pointed to the room where Mrs. Garbarini died all those years ago.

I stood in the doorway. An elderly woman, dressed in filmy pink, sat in the middle of the cramped room, on a day bed, surrounded on all sides with stacked glass cases, each containing an ornately dressed antique doll. The dead eyes all stared at her. She shook her head slowly back and forth, with a look of stark terror on her face.

I turned to my grandmother; she was still smiling. She pointed to the center of the Zone, to the black column, and I finally understood.

The rent opened by the C-bomb is closing tonight. The children of the Zone have gathered, all who could make it back, all who have always been here.

We are going home, and maybe Leah will be there waiting for me, just on the other side.

Author Bios

A. Henry Keene writes and edits from his home in Louisville, Kentucky. In his writing, Henry attempts to meld pulp fiction style and content with literary concerns. His published works include a short story collection entitled "The Crooked Closet" and a novella, "Meridina." Henry co-edited "Terror Train," an anthology, which explores the train in popular imagination and the horror genre.

Dona Fox writes short stories and poetry - horror and dark fantasy infused with bits of science fiction. Coming from the Pacific Northwest, specters from the Northwest's forests, Portland's bridges and Seattle's streets may creep into her dark tales. If you are looking for an anthology with a number of authors, everybody's favorite story by Dona seems to be "Grace at the End" which you will find in Memento Mori, another favorite is "The Hero" which is in We Are Dust and Shadow. If you want a collection of Dona's stories - Dark Tales from the Den is Dona's first collection--on these dark pages there is no distinction between the living and the dead for ghosts do walk beside us and the paranormal is normal here. A touch of Lovecraft in one tale, an alien abduction in another--or was it? Facts blend with fiction so easily in the Dark. Settle in with a Smoky Martini and end up in The Darkest Den.

Maria Mitchell is a writer and illustrator. Her work is published in the anthologies Cthulhurotica, Candle in the Attic Window, Future Lovecraft, Ugly Babies vol. 1, Demonic Possession, The Grays and Lovecraft After Dark. She has poems published in Sage Woman Magazine and artwork published in Expanded Horizons. She has short fiction published in Deadman's Tome, Fried Fiction and Yester Year Fiction. She lives in California.

Sebastian Crow is a lifelong resident of Indiana. He has been writing poetry for over thirty years and recently turned his hand to prose. He currently resides in Centerville, Indiana with his wife of twenty years and large menagerie of furry children. He loves horror, clowns and all things Ramone. "Loving the Dead" was influenced by the Nine Inch Nails song "Starfuckers, Inc." and Alice Cooper's "I Love the Dead."

Justin Hunter has five published novels and over thirty short stories in anthologies. Check out his Amazon.com author page at http://www.amazon.com/Justin-Hunter/e/B007PRBUHS. Connect him on Facebook to keep updated on upcoming releases.

Jennifer Lemming: After writing poetry for 10 years, the muse decided I needed to write some genre fiction. My story, The Charmer, was a lovely gift, sharped by literary labor, shared with anticipation, and very happily published in this anthology with a wonderful quality of writing.

Guy Burtenshaw lives in a small town in southern England and has been writing horror and crime stories for many years. He has published several horror novels and his short stories can be found in various magazines and anthologies.

K.Z. Morano is a writer, a beach bum, and a chocolate addict. She writes anything from romance and erotica to horror and SF, F, and WTF. Her stories have appeared in various anthologies, magazines and online venues. "100 Nightmares" is her first horror story collection-- a book with 100 stories, each written in 100 words, with over 50 illustrations. Visit her Facebook page https://www.facebook.com/100Nightmares

Roger Cowin (1964) was born in New Castle, Indiana. He has been working with the mentally ill for the past twenty-five years. He began writing poetry and short stories in high school before deciding to concentrate on poetry. His poetry is inspired by the wide expanses of the Mid-west and the inner landscape of its inhabitants. Balancing between the absurd and the rational, Cowin attempts to make sense of the complexities of our modern world. Equal amounts satire, anger and wry humor, Roger Cowin's poetry is both thought provoking and accessible to the general reader.

Mike Jansen has published flash fiction, short stories and longer work in various anthologies and magazines in the Netherlands and Belgium, including Cerberus, Manifesto Bravado, Wonderwaan, Ator Mondis and Babel-SF and Verschijnsel anthologies such as Ragnarok and Zwarte Zielen (Black Souls). He lives in the Netherlands, in Hilversum, near Amsterdam. He has won awards for best new author and best author in the King Kong Award in 1991 and 1992 respectively as well as an honorable mention for a submission to the Australian Altair Magazine launch competition in 1998. In 2012 Mike won awards in the SaBi Thor story contest, the Literary Prize for the Baarn Cultural Festival and the prestigious Fantastels award for best short story. More recent publications in various English language ezines and anthologies, among which several publications with JWKfiction.com, Encounters Magazine and others. For a full list please refer to Mike's site: http://www.meznir.com Mike's debut novel, 'The Failing God', will be available, in English, during 2013.

Bas van deR Veer: Besides working as a free lance Delphi coder, Bas enjoys role-playing with his friends and hard-core computer gaming. Inspired by the various worlds he encounters there, he sometimes tries his hand at writing stories. For a contest called the Fantasy Strijd Brugge he finished his first ever short story and made it to the top 10% spots.

Alec Cizak: My work has appeared in several journals and anthologies, including *Beat to a Pulp*, *Thuglit*, and *CrimeSpree*. I've recently had two books published--*Crooked Roads*, a collection of short stories, and *Between Juarez and El Paso*, a "Drifter Detective" novella. I am also the editor of the literary journal *Pulp Modern*.

Mary Patterson Thornburg: My short fiction has been published in several print and online magazines, including *Cicada; Zahir; Strange, Weird, and Wonderful;* and *Fantasy & Science Fiction*, in both volumes of *A Big Book of Strange, Weird, and Wonderful*, and in the UK anthology *Dreamless Roads*. Two of my novels (*A Glimmer of Guile* and *The Kura*) are published as e-books by Uncial Press, and both are available in print through Amazon CreateSpace.

Two of my short stories received honorable mention in *The Year's Best Fantasy and Horror* (2006, 2008), and "Niam's Tale," in the July-August 2010 *Cicada*, won the 2011 SCBWI Magazine Merit Honor Certificate.

Flo Stanton's stories, poetry and artwork have appeared in the horror anthologies *Gothic Tales of Terror, Traps, Tales of a Woman Scorned, A Pint of Bloody Fiction, Indiana Horror Review 2012, Whispers of Wickedness, Static Movement, Yellow Mama, Black Petals*, and others. Her book reviews, literary articles, and true crime pieces have been featured in *The Indianapolis Star, Castle Rock, Literally, True Police, Indiana Crime Review 2013* and *2014*, the *Futures Mystery Anthology Magazine* website, etc. She lives in Indianapolis with her writer/photographer husband John. You can find them stalking abandoned warehouses, factories, graveyards, and other haunted sites seeking macabre inspiration. Find out more about Flo at www.3amblue.com or follow her blog at http://flo-stanton.blogspot.com/

John D. Stanton's photography, poetry, articles and fiction have appeared in The Indianapolis Star, Not One of Us, MIND, Black Petals, Mt. Zion Speculative Fiction Review, Requiem for the Damned, Shadow and Substance, RAZAR I and II, Yellow Mama, Theatre of Decay, Static Movement, and many other publications. In the visual realm, his specialties include historic photo restoration, infrared photography, and stereography. His unique Subtractive Illusion, a stereoscopic demonstration involving color-tint frequencies that cancel each other out in the brain, is featured on Corel.com. During the years John was an IT consultant and ran a DTP business, his articles were published in Computer User, Compuserve Magazine, ST World and ST Express. He also edited various computer newsletters. John has provided hundreds of images to the small press, electronic and print editions and book covers, earning Top Ten Finisher in the annual Preditor and Editor polls, as well as three mentions in Ellen Datlow's "Best of" collections. John taught an editing class at Marian University with his wife Flo. The two artists stalk abandoned warehouses, factories, graveyards, and other haunted sites where they find bizarre inspiration for their photographic, audio, and literary creations.

NOW AVAILABLE

NOW AVAILABLE

www.ingramcontent.com/pod-product-compliance
Lightning Source LLC
Chambersburg PA
CBHW070554180626
46817CB00005B/1837